Twisted Beautiee 3
An Erotic Thriller

Twisted Beautiee 3
An Erotic Thriller

BY

TRACY WILSON

http://beautifulpublications.com

Published by
Beautiful Publications LLC
Stratford, CT 06614

PRINT ISBN: 978-0-9985765-8-9
EBOOK ISBN: 978-1-7331792-8-7

Printed in the United States of America

Dedication

I dedicate this series to my alter ego, Beautiee.

Chapter 1

"Good morning – Osgood Publishing – how may I help you?"

"Good morning Joselyn," I said.

"How are you Mrs. Osgood?" she greeted.

"Not too good – I need you to set up an emergency meeting with the Board of Directors – let Samuel know everyone needs to drop everything – I'll be there at 10," I said as I started getting dressed.

"I'll get right on it Mrs. Osgood – see you at 10."

"Good morning," I greeted as I walked into the Board Room and headed to the head of the table. Thank you all for coming – I'll get right to it. Last night, my husband was shot. He was rushed into emergency surgery at Milford Hospital..." I paused to gather myself as everyone gasped and whispered. I waited for the room to quiet down before I continued... "He came out of surgery but, unfortunately... he's in a comma. At this time, we don't know if he's going to make it..." I paused again to keep from crying and to also give everyone in the room time to adjust to hearing the devastating news... "Effective immediately – Samuel Logan, Vice President, will

1

be acting President and CEO. Everything goes through him and, in turn, he will run everything by me. If there's an emergency and I cannot be reached, Samuel has the final say. Are there any questions?" I asked as Sheila Henley, CFO (Chief Financial Officer) walked in...

"Sorry I'm late..." she said as she closed the door... "What'd I miss?"

"You're fired." I stated. Everyone gasped.

"Excuse me?"

"You're fired – clean out your desk – you have one hour." Sheila exited the room in a huff, closed the door, and I continued... "Are there any questions?" No one answered. Some of the board members acknowledged what I said by shaking their head no. "Very well – thank you for coming." The board members filed out one by one. After everyone left the room, Samuel spoke...

"Mrs. Osgood?"

"Yes Samuel?"

"If you don't mind... I'd like you to reconsider your decision to fire Sheila..."

"Why?"

"We need her... she can't be easily replaced..."

"Are you saying you can't do her job in the interim?"

"I could... it's just that the quarterly reports are due and we have a responsibility to the shareholders..."

"My husband could die at any moment – and I'm here – do you really think I don't know we have a responsibility to the shareholders?"

"You're right – I'm sorry..."

"Go get Sheila," I commanded...

"Yes Mrs. Osgood..." Samuel said as he went to get Sheila..."

"Yes Mrs. Osgood?" Sheila sniffed as she sat down. I looked at her and I could tell she'd been crying...

"What's going on with you?" I asked.

"I'm sorry Mrs. Osgood... my kids..."

"Let me stop you right there!" I snapped. My husband is in the hospital in a comma – he may not make it – and I'm here – do you understand what I'm saying?"

"Yes Mrs. Osgood... sorry about your husband..."

"Samuel asked me to reconsider my decision to fire you because you're valuable and can't be easily replaced," I said as I looked at Samuel...

"Thank you Sam," she said.

"Here's what I need you to do – go home – handle whatever it is you need to handle – and come back tomorrow – but I need you to understand if life happens and you have an emergency – you are to notify us as soon as possible so we are aware – and don't ever walk in late to a board meeting again and ask what'd I miss – is that understood?"

"Yes Mrs. Osgood."

"Okay Sheila – see you tomorrow..."

"Mrs. Osgood..." Joselyn huffed out of breath as she ran into the conference room...

"Yes Joselyn – what's wrong?"

"The police are here – they asked me where you were..."

"It's okay Joselyn – get Attorney Smalls on the phone – have him meet me at the station – tell him I'm being arrested!" I yelled as Joselyn hurried... "Yes Mrs. Osgood!" she yelled as she ran down the hall...

"Mrs. Osgood?" Katina said as she walked over to me with Sergeant Chandler...

"I am..." I said as I stood up...

"We need you to come with us..." Katina said as she went to grab me by the arm...

"Excuse me!" I said as I snatched my arm away from her...

"Mrs. Osgood... please..." Sergeant Chandler asked...

"You said you need me to come with you – I'm quite capable of walking by my damn self!" I snapped as they escorted me out to the squad car.

"This way please," Katina ordered as I was escorted into the Milford City Police Department in Milford, Connecticut.

"How romantic..." I sighed.

"Excuse me?" Katina snapped...

"Well..." I laughed, "When my husband comes out of his comma... we'll be celebrating a few things... one of which will be that we both got arrested... by you!" I laughed hysterically...

"I can't wich y'all – somebody get her and process her..."

"Umm... Detective?" I asked, getting her attention...

"Yes?"

"I am under arrest... right?"

"That's correct..."

"Well..."

"What is it Mrs. Osgood?"

"Are you going to Mirandize me?"

"Oh God... is it 5:00 yet?" she sighed...

"It's always 5:00 somewhere," I laughed, enjoying the fact that she was annoyed...

"Beautiee Osgood... I'm placing you under arrest..."

"Hot Damn! What are the charges?"

"You're being charged with the attempted murder of Bazil Osgood, the murder of Sonia Santos, and the murder of Trevor Joseph..."

"Awww Shit! A Trifecta! Ahhh! Haaa! Haaa!" I laughed...

"What's going on here?" Sergeant Chandler yelled as he came down the hall...

"She thinks this is a fuckin' joke!" Katina snapped...

"That's it – get your ass over here," he said as he came towards me...

"You put your fuckin' hands on me and I'll bury your ass!" I screamed...

"Oh so you gangsta now?" he laughed...

"She's not – but you already know I am," Attorney Smalls said as he walked in...

"Look Smalls," Sergeant Chandler said...

"I'ma need you to step away from my client... have you been Mirandized yet Beautiee?"

"I was trying to do that but your client thinks this is a fuckin' joke!" Katina snapped.

"She's right – it is!" Attorney Smalls laughed, "But you don't need me to remind you that if you don't Mirandize her, you're violating her rights... and I get paid by the hour... so what we doin'?"

"Sigh..." Katina breathed as she began to give me the Miranda warning:

1. You have the right to remain silent.
2. Anything you say can and will be used against you in a court of law.
3. You have the right to an attorney.
4. If you cannot afford an attorney one will be provided for you.
5. Do you understand the rights I have just read to you?"

"I do," I said as I tried to take her hand but she snatched it away...

"With these rights in mind, do you wish to speak to me?"

"Hell no!" Attorney Smalls laughed before I could answer...

"C'mon..." Katina said as she took me for processing. Attorney Smalls met me in the attorney/client room afterwards...

"Beautiee... we need to talk..."

"I know..." I said as I sat down...

"These are some serious charges..."

"I know..."

"I'll defend you with everything I have — but I need to know everything..."

"I know..."

"This is serious... you makin' a joke out there..."

"I laugh to keep from crying..." I interrupted.

"Are you okay?"

"Hell no!"

"You need anything?"

"I need a drink..."

"The best I can do is coffee — I'll be right back," he said as he left to go get me coffee. I sat there at the table staring off into nowhere...

"How in the hell did I get here?" I asked out loud.

"Here Beautiee," Attorney Smalls said as he sat down with two cups of coffee... "Did you give them a statement?"

"Keisha and Troy did," I answered.

"Who's Keisha and Troy?"

"My neighbors... and my friends... I answered as I teared up...

"You're gonna get through this Beautiee... I gotchu..." he said as he came over to me and gave me a hug. "Let me sit here," he said as he pulled the chair up beside me..."

"If it weren't for Keisha and Troy – I'da been alone..." I said as I started to cry...

"Beautiee?"

"Yes?"

"Did they both give a statement to the police?"

"They both talked to Katina," I answered.

"Do you know what they said?"

"No..." I answered as he handed me some tissues...

"Do I need to be concerned about their statements?"

"No."

"Okay – I'll get a copy of them anyway – what happened at the hospital?"

"They swabbed me for blood samples and they took pictures..."

"Uh huh... what else?"

"They wanted to do a rape kit but I refused..."

"Did you tell them you were raped?"

"No."

"Did they ask you if you were raped?"

"Yes."

"What did you tell them?"

"I told them I wasn't raped."

"Okay – just so we're clear – you were not raped?"

"No – I was not raped..."

"Why the fuck did they want to do a rape kit then?"

"I'on know — maybe because I was covered in blood..."

"Hold on... let me look at these pictures... Oh shit! They didn't let you put any clothes on?"

"I didn't have any to put on..."

"Wait — you mean your friends didn't bring you any clothes?"

"There wasn't any time."

"Wait — how the fuck..."

"After Bazil was shot — they took him out on the stretcher — Troy gave me a robe to put on — I ran out the house, pushed Detective Jones out my way — and screamed for Bazil..." I explained as I cried... "Thank God they heard me screaming or I wouldn't have made it into the ambulance..." I said as I cried on his shoulder..."

"Hmmmmm... you weren't charged with assaulting an officer... I'm surprised... she actually did you a solid..."

"She didn't do shit!" I screamed... "She saw me running to get in the ambulance with Bazil and she tried to stop me — Fuckin' Bitch!"

"Calm down... I know you're upset — but that is something in your favor..." he said as he took notes... "I need to know what happened... from the beginning..."

"Okay..." I sighed... then finished my coffee... "I invited Sonia over to have sex with me so my husband could watch us and then join in..."

"Uh Huh..." he said as he wrote down what I said...

"That's all you have to say?"

"What am I supposed to say?"

"I'on know... I thought you'd be surprised..."

"I'll be surprised later... continue..."

"Okay... so Sonia agreed to come over..."

"Did Sonia know your husband would be there?"

"Yes."

"And she consented?"

"Yes."

"Okay – continue..."

"So Bazil was watching us have sex... then he joined in..."

"Was that consensual?"

"Yes."

"Did he have sex with both of you?"

"No – just me."

"So – to be clear – Bazil never touched Sonia?"

"Bazil never touched Sonia..."

"Okay – continue..."

"I saw the gun..."

"What gun?"

"I yelled for Bazil to look out but it was too late... he shot Bazil..."

"Who shot Bazil?"

"Trevor shot Bazil..." I answered as I cried...

"Okay – continue..."

"I grabbed Sonia and held her down on top of me... Trevor pointed the gun at me – but he hit Sonia instead..." I cried...

"Okay... then what happened?"

"Trevor screamed Sonia's name... and dropped the gun on the floor... and that's when I realized Sonia set us up..." I cried...

"Sonia set you up?"

"She had to! The only ones that new Sonia was invited over were me and Bazil!" I cried...

"How did Trevor get in your house?"

"I'on know!"

"Okay, okay - what happened next?"

"Trevor came over to Sonia... he started holding her... then he told me it was all my fault and she didn't deserve to die... so I picked up the gun before he could... and I shot him..."

"Oh shit!"

"He tried to shoot me first! It was self-defense!"

"I agree with you... but the defense will argue..."

"They'll argue that I should have let him pick up the gun and try again?"

"You have a point..."

"Exactly..."

"So – to be clear – Trevor was not invited to your house?"

"No."

"And – to be clear – you have no idea how Trevor got in your house?"

"No."

"Where was Trevor when he shot Bazil?"

"He was in my bedroom..."

"He was in your bedroom? And he wasn't invited?"

"No – I never, ever, invited Trevor to my house..."

"Okay Beautiee – I need to ask you something..."

"Okay..."

"Do you have any idea why Trevor would want to kill you or Bazil?"

"I know exactly why Trevor wanted us dead..."

"Why?"

"Because... Bazil and Trevor were lovers..."

"Whhhaaaattt!?"

"Bazil and Trevor were lovers – is that going to come out in court?"

"Yes..."

"Oh well..."

"So... if they were lovers... why did he want y'all dead?"

"Because... Bazil told him it was over between them..."

"Wait – Trevor wanted to kill Bazil because Bazil broke up with him... to be with you?"

"Yes..."

"Damn..." he sighed as he continued taking notes... "Is there anything else I need to know?"

"Yes..."

"Okay..."

"Bazil and Trevor have been lovers since they were in prison together..."

"I'm glad you're telling me this – that prosecuting attorney is a real Bitch – she likes to pull surprises – I'm glad we'll be one up on her ass... okay... take a look at this and tell me what you think..." he said as he pushed the pad over to me with a statement...

"I invited Sonia to my house to have sex while my husband watched. The sex was consensual. Sonia and I were having sex and my husband joined in. While we were having sex, I saw the gun and yelled for Bazil to watch out, but he couldn't move fast enough and was shot. Trevor pointed the gun at me to shoot me but because Sonia was on top of me, he shot her instead. Trevor dropped the gun on the floor, ran over to Sonia, told me it was all my fault, and Sonia didn't deserve to die. At that point, I feared for my life so I picked the gun up off the floor and shot Trevor."

"How's that?" he asked as I read it... I couldn't answer him right away... I just burst into tears...

"I'll sign it..."

"Okay – once you sign this – don't answer any questions..."

"Okay..."

"You'll be in here for tonight – but I'll get you out of here first thing tomorrow – can you make bail?"

"I'll put up my house..."

13

"You can't put up your house... it's in Bazil's name..."

"I said I'll put up 'MY' house..."

"Your house?"

"Yes... in Bridgeport..."

"Okay – hang in there Beautiee..." he said as he hugged me... "You ready?"

"Yea... I'm ready..." I said as I signed the statement...

"We're ready," he said after opening the door...

"Is your client ready to make a statement?" Katina asked as she sat down at the table...

"Here's her statement," he said as he pushed it to her...

"Really?" she said as she started reading it...

"That's her statement."

"This some bullshit!"

"That's up to the prosecutor."

"Whatever..." she said as she stood up... "I just want this day to be over... come with me Beautiee..."

"May I have a moment with my attorney?"

"Sigh..." she breathed as she left the room and stood outside...

"Thank you," I whispered as I gave him a hug..."

"You're welcome," he said as he tried to pull away...

"Get the surveillance..." I whispered in his ear as Katina came back into the room...

"Are you done?"

"Yes..."

"C'mon..." she said as I followed her to the holding cell.

Chapter 2

"Good morning Your Honor," Attorney Smalls said as we went into the courtroom.

"Not really – let's get this over with – I've got a hell of a day ahead of me," she said as she sat on the Bench...

"Good morning Your Honor," the prosecuting attorney said as she stood up. "We're requesting Mrs. Osgood be held without bail due to the charges..."

"Beverly..." Attorney Smalls interrupted.

"Please address your comments to the court!" the Judge snapped.

"Yes Your Honor..." Attorney Smalls said. "Your Honor, my client's husband is in Milford Hospital in a medical comma. At this time she isn't going anywhere but the hospital. I'm requesting that she be released on her own recognizance..."

"You're kidding right?" Beverly laughed. "Attorney Smalls, you're clients been charged with the attempted murder of her husband as well as two additional murders – you can't really expect your client to get off with a slap on the wrist," she laughed.

16

"Thank you Your Honor," Beverly said.

"Don't thank me just yet," the judge said. "I agree the charges are serious, but I also agree that Mrs. Osgood shouldn't be held without bail. As heinous as the crimes are, Mrs. Osgood has no prior convictions – not even a parking ticket. I believe if I set bail, Attorney Smalls will ensure his client will come to court."

"Absolutely Your Honor," Attorney Smalls acknowledged.

"Very well... I'm setting bail at $200,000."

"Make sure you remind your client she can't use her husband's house to make bail," Beverly laughed as she walked out the court room...

"Don't worry about her – I'll take care of this right way – wait here," Attorney Smalls said as he went to give the Mortgage Statement, Deed, and Title information to the Bail Agent.

"Beautiee..." Keisha called as she came running into the court room...

"Hey Keisha..." I said as I got up to hug her...

"I can't stay long – I'm out to lunch – here's your clothes..."

"Thank you Keisha – I love you – kiss Troy for me..."

"I will!" she yelled as she ran out the courtroom.

"You ready?" Attorney Smalls asked as he came to take my hand...

"Yes I am!" I said as I stood up.

"Where can I take you?"

"To the ladies' room... so I can get dressed for my husband!" I answered with a smile as we walked down the hall...

"I like that," he said.

"What?"

"Seeing you smile."

"Thanks..." I said as I went into the bathroom... and broke down crying. I didn't even bother going into the stall – I just stopped right there in front of the sink – I was so happy to be out of that jumpsuit...

"Oh my God – excuse me – why didn't you use a stall?" the lady said as she came in...

"I didn't want to... I like seeing myself in the mirror..."

"Whatever," she said as she went to the bathroom, flushed the toilet, and ran out without washing her hands...

"I guess she couldn't stand the sight of me..." I laughed as I got dressed. Keisha new me well. She picked out one of my favorite outfits – the same outfit Bazil picked out for me the night he proposed. "I'm coming Bazil..." I said as I hurried out the bathroom...

"Well look at you!" Attorney Smalls said as he looked me up and down...

"Look at me!" I beamed.

"Where's the jumpsuit?"

"In the garbage!" I laughed as he took my arm and led me out the courthouse. When I saw the parking lot, I dropped down on my knees and kissed the ground. After he watched me get up, he opened his car door, made sure I was secure, and took me straight to the hospital...

"Mrs. Osgood – thank God – we've been trying to reach you!" Dr. Preston breathed.

"Sorry – I was in jail..."

"You want me to stay Beautiee?" Attorney Smalls asked.

"Please... what's wrong Doctor Preston?"

"I actually have good news..."

"Oh thank God!" I breathed.

"I'm taking your husband off the ventilator..." he said... and then paused...

"What's wrong Doctor Preston?"

"While your husband was in a comma we needed to use a stronger sedative. Normally we use Propofol but because your husband was so weak, we used Midazolam which is a Benzodiazepine. The longer the stronger sedative is used, the greater the chance of you becoming addicted to it. If we take him off the sedative too soon, he may go through withdrawal and his liver and kidney function may be impaired and we need to make sure they're at full capacity."

"Will my husband wake up?"

"Yes – he will definitely wake up – it's just going to take a bit longer. I'm going to wean him off gradually so when he does wake up, he won't go through withdrawal and his liver and kidneys will function normally."

"Thank you Doctor Preston," I said as I grabbed him into a hug and cried.

"You're welcome – I've got to get to surgery – any questions – go see Nurse Trinity!" he said as he ran down the hall...

"Well alright!" Attorney Smalls said as he hugged me...

"He's gonna be okay... he's gonna be okay..." I cried.

"I told you!"

"Yes you did!" I said as I pulled him into another hug...

"I need to get back to court – call me if you need me..." he said as he turned to leave...

"I will... thank you!"

"You're welcome!" he yelled as he left.

"Hi Trinity!" I beamed as I got to the nurses station...

"Heeeyyy! You look great!" she said as she hugged me...

"I feel great too..." I said.

"I guess you're here to see your husband..." she said as I followed her down the hall to his room.

"Hey my Thirst Quencher..." I whispered in his ear when I got up close to him... "I love you..." I said as I kissed him. I saw the monitors spike a bit, smiled, climbed in the bed with him, pulled up the covers, took his dick out of his pajamas, and played with his dick until I fell asleep.

3 Months Later...

"Hey my Thirst Quencher," I breathed as I plopped down in the chair. The interior designer I hired really outdid herself in making this look like a bedroom. "I've had a long day so I'm going to jump in the shower right quick... I'll be right back," I said as I stripped out of my clothes and walked into the shower...

"I wish this Bitch would realize we're not her personal maids," Thelma said as she began picking up my clothes...

"Which Bitch would you be referring to?" I asked as I came out the shower..."

"Ooohhh... Hi Mrs. Osgood... I didn't realize you were here..."

"Well now that you know I'm here, you can leave!" I snapped.

"I need to make sure your husband..."

"Get out!" I yelled as the Nurse Trinity came down the hall and into the room...

"Is everything okay in here Mrs. Osgood?" I noticed how she glared at Thelma and Thelma looked terrified. As much as I enjoyed this I started thinking Thelma might actually need her job after all...

"Yes... everything's fine," I lied. "I was just coming out of the shower and didn't realize anyone was in the room," I lied again.

"Will you be staying with your husband tonight?" she asked.

"Yes, I'll be staying tonight," I answered.

"Well, we'll give you some privacy... If you need anything at all, just let us know..." she said as she started pushing Thelma out the room...

"I sure swill," I laughed as I closed the door behind them, making sure to lock it... "Finally!" I said as I climbed into bed with Bazil and snuggled down next to him... "I miss you sooo much," I whispered in his ear as I started playing with his dick..." Meanwhile... at the Nurse's Station...

"Nurse Trinity? You need to come take a look at this..." Nurse Yvonne Williams said.

"What's wrong?"

"Bazil's heart rate and pulse is increasing..."

"I know..."

"Do you think we should tell Dr. Preston?"

"That won't be necessary Yvonne."

"Shouldn't the doctor know?"

"Trust me Yvonne... he knows..."

"Are you sure?"

"You're new here right?"

"Yea..."

"Well... let me explain what's going on there... every time Mrs. Osgood spends the night with her husband... his heart rate and pulse spikes..."

"Aaawww... that's so sweet..." Nurse Yvonne sighed.

"Trinity..." Nurse Tisha laughed "Just tell her already... I can't take it..."

"I don't understand..." Nurse Yvonne said...

"She's playing with his dick," Nurse Trinity said as Nurse Trinity and Nurse Tisha bust out laughing...

"Oh my God! You mean they're having sex?" Nurse Yvonne squealed...

"Yes Chille!" Nurse Tisha laughed.

"But how? He's in a comma!" Nurse Yvonne exclaimed.

"Yes he is... but it's quite normal..." Nurse Trinity explained...

"It is? Oh wow..." Nurse Yvonne whispered.

"Happens all the time around here," Nurse Tisha laughed...

"I don't understand... how do you get an erection in a comma?" Nurse Yvonne asked...

"By the grace of God Honey..." Nurse Trinity answered as they laughed. Meanwhile... back in the Bazil's room...

"Beautiee..."

"Yes my Thirst Quencher..." I answered as I continued playing with his dick, falling asleep on Love it or List It..."

"Beautiee..." Bazil moaned again...

"Bazil?" I jumped up, climbed on top of him, and held him up...

"Beautiee..."

"Yes my Thirst Quencher..." I moaned as I sat on his dick and began riding...

"Beautiee..." he moaned as he grabbed my ass and held on tight... Meanwhile... back at the nurse's station...

"Nurse Trinity?"

"Yes Nurse Yvonne?"

"Umm... I know what you said but..."

"Le'me take a look," Nurse Trinity said as she interrupted Nurse Yvonne... "Oh shit – get Dr. Preston – STAT!" Nurse Trinity yelled...

"Okay!" Nurse Yvonne said as she grabbed the phone ... "Dr. Preston... you need to get here right away... Mr. Osgood's numbers are spiraling... I don't know... hold on... he wants to talk to you..." Nurse Yvonne said as she handed Nurse Trinity the phone...

"Yes Dr. Preston?" Nurse Trinity answered as she grabbed the phone... Okay... right away Dr. Preston," Nurse Trinity said as they all ran down the hall towards Bazil's room. Meanwhile... back in Bazil's room...

"I missed this pussy..." Bazil moaned as I continued riding..."

"Oh Bazil... it's been so long..." I moaned.

"Cum with me..."

"I'm cummmmmmiiiinnnnggg..... Bazil..."

"MmmmMmmmph...MmmmMmmmph... MmmmMmmmph...

"Aaaaaggghhhhh...." I screamed as they broke the door to Bazils room...

"Oh my God! She's trying to kill him!" Nurse Yvonne yelled as they all burst into the room...

"Oh my God... Mrs. Osgood... I'm so embarrassed..." Nurse Trinity said as she and Nurse Tisha stood in the room...

"Chille... what's a matter with you... you ain't never caught your parent's fuckin' before?" Nurse Tisha laughed as she pushed Nurse Trinity and Nurse Yvonne out of Bazil's room...

"Dr. Preston's on his way... I'll hold him at the nurse's station until you're ready for him to come in," she laughed as she closed the door...

"You didn't leave me..." Bazil whispered with tears in his eyes..."

"I made you a promise..." I said as we kissed...

"I'm so sorry Beautiee..."

"I love you my Thirst Quencher..."

"I love you too..."

"I need to get dressed... before we end up putting on another show," I laughed as I got up off of him....

"Beautiee..."

"I'll be right there my Thirst Quencher... just let me finish getting dressed...

"Beautiee..."

"Yes my Thirst Quencher... OH MY GOD!!! BAZIL!!!!" I screamed as Dr. Preston came rushing into the room with Nurse Trinity...

"Mrs. Osgood... we need you to leave... Dr. Preston said as he pushed past me along with Nurse Trinity... "On three... One... Two... Three!" Dr. Preston yelled as he tried to revive Bazil with the defibrillator... "Again! On three... One... Two... Three!" Dr. Preston yelled again as he tried again to revive Bazil with the defibrillator to no avail... "Again!"

"Dr. Preston..." Nurse Trinity whispered...

"I said again! On three... One... Two... Three!" Dr. Preston yelled as he tried one last time to revive Bazil with the defibrillator... "Call it..." he breathed.

"11:30 p.m." Nurse Trinity said.

"I'm so sorry Mrs. Osgood," Dr. Preston said as he put his hand on my shoulder... and I collapsed to the floor... "Nurse... get her up here on this stretcher... STAT!"

"BAZIL? BAZIL? BAZIL? WHERE ARE YOU?" I cried...

"Beautiee?"

"Bazil!"

"Beautiee? Are you really here?" he asked as tears streamed down his face...

"Yes my Thirst Quencher... I'm here," I answered, crying as we embraced...

"Beautiee... you need to go back..."

"I made you a promise..."

"Till death do us part Beautiee..."

"I never promised you that..."

"What did you promise me then?"

"When I married you... I promised you I'd love you forever..." I answered as I wrapped my arm around him...

"Yes... yes you did..." he said as we walked are in arm towards the light...

"Beautiee..."

"Yes Lord?"

"You need to go back..."

"I can't live without Bazil..." I cried as I held on to him as tight as I could...

"Yes you can my child..."

"No... I can't..."

"Who am I Beautiee?"

"Father God," I answered lowering my head.

"Look at me Beautiee," God commanded, lifting my head up by my chin. It was so bright... all I could see where the most beautiful blue eyes... "Where is your faith? Where is your trust?"

"Right here in front of you," I whispered as I cried.

"Show me..." God commanded...

"Yes Lord," I whispered as I let go of Bazil...

"BEAUTIEE!" Bazil cried as I disappeared through the tunnel..."

"BAZIL!" God boomed.

"Yes God," Bazil whispered.

"Do you know why you're here?"

"To be honest... I thought I'd be in hell..."

"Don't try me Bazil... you still could be...

"I'm sorry God..."

"I know..."

"You know?"

"Who am I Bazil?"

"My bad... You're God..."

"You should have died a long time ago Bazil..."

"I know God..."

"Yet... you're still here... by my Grace..."

"I know..."

"You let me down Bazil..."

"I know God... I'm sorry..." Bazil said as tears streamed down his face...

"I know you are son..."

"Please God..." Bazil cried as he dropped to his knees... "Don't make Beautiee live without me..."

"She'll be just fine," God answered.

"Pleaseeeee..." Bazil cried...

"I've waited your whole life for you to come to me Bazil..."

"I know God... but I couldn't..."

"You're coming to me now..."

"I know... but this is different..."

"Because you need me?"

"Yeesss..." Bazil whispered.

"Why do you think Beautiee chose you?"

"Because I love her."

"And how do you think you wound up at that hotel?"

"Oh My God!"

"Yes Bazil... Oh Your God..."

"Thank you God...Thank you..." Bazil cried...

"You're welcome... and Bazil?"

"Yes God?"

"Don't ever hurt Beautiee again...."

"I won't God... I promise... and..."

"You never make a promise you can't keep... I know, I know," God laughed as he sent Bazil back to me...

"We've got a pulse!" Dr. Preston yelled as I opened my eyes...

"Welcome back," Nurse Trinity said as she wiped my forehead.

"I love you Bazil," I whispered as tears fell down my cheeks...

"I love you too..."

"Bazil?" I shrieked as I jumped up off the stretcher and turned to look...

"Holy shit!" Dr. Preston exclaimed... "How the fuck... Nurse Trinity - get me the neuro surgeon... now!"

"I'm on it Dr. Preston!" Nurse Trinity yelled as she ran down the hall to the nurse's station...

"What's going on?" Nurse Tisha yelled.

"He's alive! Dr. Remi...Dr. Remi!"

"What's wrong Nurse Trinity?" Dr. Remi asked as he came running...

"He's alive! He's alive!" she yelled as she grabbed him and pulled him to Bazil's room...

"Bazil Osgood!" Dr. Remi exclaimed when he saw Bazil... "Mrs. Osgood, we need to do an MRI and a CAT scan to see if your husband suffered any brain damage...

"He's fine," I sighed.

"We can't be sure of that until we run tests Mrs. Osgood...

"You may not be sure... but I am," I said as I held Bazil's hand....

"He's alive?" Nurse Yvonne asked as she came into the room...

"He's alive," Dr. Preston answered. "I still can't believe it..."

"How many miracles do you need to witness before you know God is real?" Dr. Remi asked.

"Here we go again with the bullshit..." Dr. Preston said... "This can all be explained by modern science... he probably still had brain activity after we declared him dead... I wish you'd stop trying to convince me...

"Doctor Preston?" I interrupted.

"Yes Mrs. Osgood?"

"Dr. Remi isn't trying to convince you of anything... God is," I said.

"Tell him Chille," Nurse Tisha said.

"Look Mrs. Osgood... I'm happy for you... but I'd appreciate it if you'd..."

"Doctor Preston?"

"Yes Mrs. Osgood?"

"As long as you live... you'll continue to witness miracles... whether you believe in God or not," I said matter-of-factly...

"I give up!" Doctor Preston laughed.

"C'mon... let's get your husband down to MRI," Dr. Remi said... "The sooner we get these results back, the sooner your husband can go home.

"Amen!" I said.

"C'mon Mr. Osgood – let's get you down to MRI – it'll take about an hour or so – then we'll see," Dr. Remi said as he pushed the bed down the hall towards MRI...

"I'll get the results from Dr. Remi Mrs. Osgood – if everything's ckay, I'll see your husband in two weeks," Dr. Preston said as he left the room.

"You're finally going home," Nurse Trinity said.

"Yes we are – I'll be back in a bit..." I said as I ran out the hospital, jumped in the car, and headed straight home...

"Hey Beautiee – how's Bazil?" Troy asked...

"He's coming home today – I gotta go – I'll call y'all later..." I said as I opened the door and ran upstairs... "Shit – where is it?" I said out loud as I looked through the closet... "Got it!" I yelled as I grabbed his clothes, grabbed his ring, ran out the door to the car, and headed back to the hospital...

"Mrs. Osgood – you're just in time – he's good to go – but I want to see him for a follow up in 3 months..."

"Thank you Dr. Remi – where's my husband?"

"He's waiting for you in his room..."

"Thank you..." I said as I walked up to Dr. Remi... and kissed him in the mouth..."

"Mrs. Osgood... Ummm... You're welcome... I guess..." he laughed nervously...

"Mmmmmmwwwwaaa!" I said as I kissed Trinity..."

"You're welcome Beautiee..." she smiled as she hugged me...

"Thank you Tisha..." I said as I kissed her..."

"You're welcome..." she smiled... "Yvonne?"

"Yes Trinity?"

"Beautiee's taking her husband home today!"

"Congratulations!" Yvonne said as she pulled me into a hug... and I kissed her...

"Thank you Yvonne..." I laughed as Trinity and Tisha laughed with me...

"I'on know you like that for you to be kissing me..." she laughed...

"Thelma..."

"Yes Yvonne?"

"Beautiee's taking her husband home today – isn't that great?"

"It sure is – I can clean his room before I go home..." she said as she kept walking down the hall past the nurse's station...

"I see you ain't rush to kiss her ass!" Yvonne laughed.

"And I won't... I'll see y'all later..." I said as I headed to Bazil's room...

"Beautiee..." he moaned as he pulled me into a kiss..."

"Hey my Thirst Quencher..." I said as I kissed him back...

"Mmmmmm... nice cologne... who's is it?" he laughed.

"It's Doctor Remi's..." I laughed as he held me.

"You must have been pretty close to him if I can smell his cologne..." he said as he kissed me again..."

"I was..." I said as I kissed him back..."

"How close were you?" he asked as we continued kissing...

"Close enough to kiss him..."

"Did you kiss him?" he moaned as he kissed me on my neck...

"Yeeesss..." I moaned as he started massaging my breasts...

"Did you kiss anyone else?" he breathed as he pulled me to him and slipped his hand in my pants...

"I kissed them all..." I moaned as he started playing with my clit...

"Hmmmmm.... just like I remembered..." he breathed as he kissed me again...

"Bazil... get dressed... so we can go home..." I said between kisses...

"Cum for me..." Bazil growled as he continued holding me with one hand and playing with my clit with the other...

"Oooohhh..." I moaned in Bazil's mouth as he covered my mouth with his while continuing to apply pressure to my clit... "Mmmmmm.... Mmmmmm.... Mmmmmm..." I moaned in his mouth as I came all over Bazil's hand.

"Mmmmmm...." Bazil moaned as he pulled his hand out my pants and licked his fingers... "Sweet..." he said as he pulled me into a kiss...

"Hurry up Bazil..." I breathed...

"Yes Beautiee..." he said seductively as he got dressed.

"Come here my Thirst Quencher..." I commanded...

"Yes Beautiee?" he asked as he walked towards me...

"With this ring... I thee wed... again..." I cried as I put the ring on his finger...

"I love you soooo much..." Bazil cried as he pulled me into a kiss...

"I love you too... let's go..." I said as I took him by the hand and pulled him out the room...

"Mr. Osgood – wait – your discharge papers!" Nurse Trinity yelled...

"Mail 'em!" Bazil yelled as I pulled him down the corridor and outside into the parking lot...

"Get in..." I commanded as I opened the passenger side door...

"You're driving?"

"Yes — now get in!"

"Yes Maam!" Bazil laughed as he got in and closed the door...

"Finally!" I said as I got in, closed the door, and started the car...

"Ummmmmm.... Beautiee?"

"Yes my Thirst Quencher?" I answered as I buckled up and made a beeline out the parking lot...

"You okay?"

"I'm fine — I'm just hungry — where we goin' to eat?"

"Cracker Barrel..." he said as I bust out laughing...

"What's so funny?"

"We went to Cracker Barrel... when you were in the comma..."

"We?"

"Me, Troy, Keisha..." I said as I got quiet.

"I'm sorry Beautiee..."

"I told them I wanted one of everything on the menu... but it was close to closing... so we only got six plates..." I said as I started crying...

"Beautiee... pull over..."

"No..." I said as I looked straight ahead and kept driving until we got to Cracker Barrel. Bazil kept quiet until I parked the car...

"Beautiee... wait..." he said as he touched my hand...

"Yes my Thirst Quencher?" I answered...

"C'mere..." he said as he pulled me underneath his arm and held me... "Just sit here with me..." he said as he pulled me closer to him...

"Okay..." I relented...

"I liked it when you spend the night..."

"You did?"

"Of course... you played with my dick every night... why wouldn't I like that?"

"I missed you Bazil..." I sighed.

"I missed you too... I wouldn't have made it without you..." he said as he pulled me into a kiss..."

"You wouldn't have made it without God Bazil..." I said.

"Listen to me Beautiee..."

"Okay..."

"I know God saved my life... with you..." he said as he kissed me again...

"Oh Bazil..." I said as I cried...

"Most people would have gone home after visiting hours were over... but you spent every night with me... I heard you... I felt you... I smelled your hair... I fought like hell to get back to you... and you never left me... it took 3 months... and you never left me... after everything I put you through... you never left me... I don't deserve you..." he said as he cried...

"Oh yes you do... my Thirst Quencher..." I said as I kissed his tears off his face... "And I deserve you too..." I said as I kissed him again... "Now... let's go get something to eat – because the sooner we eat... the sooner we can have dessert...

"Mmmmm... dessert..." he said as he pushed me down in the front seat and laid down on top of me...

"Bazil..."

"Yes Beautiee..." he breathed as he kissed me..."

"I'm hungry..."

"So am I..." he breathed before kissing me fully in the mouth...

"Bazil..." I said between kisses... we'll get caught..."

"It's been so long... I don't care..." Bazil said as he opened my pants and pulled them down to my ankles..."

"Oh Bazil..." I moaned as he pulled his pants down enough for me to feel his ass...

"Beautiee..." he moaned as he entered me...

"Bazil... I moaned as I kicked my pants off my ankles, spread my legs, grabbed his ass, and pushed him in deeper...

"Ugghh! Ugghh! Ugghh!" Bazil growled in my ear as he thrust harder and deeper..."

"Bazil... Bazil... Bazil..." I moaned as I put one leg up on the back of the seat...

"Gimmie that pussy... Fuuuuccckkk!!!!"

"Bazzzziiillll!   I'm cuuummmmmiiinnnggg!" I screamed as I dug my fingers into his ass...

"Beautiee..." Bazil breathed as he collapsed on top of me, kissing me...

"Bazil..." I breathed in between kisses... "That was so fucking good..."

"Indeed..."

"I'm hungry..."

"You want more..."

"Yeeesss... I want more..."

"Okay... let's go eat... and when we get home... I'll give you as much as you want..."

"Promise?" I breathed as we continued kissing...

"Promise..." he breathed as he kissed me again...

"Thank God we're not parked in front of the restaurant..." I laughed as we got dressed and got out the car.

"You're back!" the waitress said as we walked in. "Are your friends joining you?"

"No... it's just us tonight..." Bazil answered as he pulled me into a kiss...

"Date night?" she asked...

"Something like that..." Bazil answered.

"Well... I hope you get my table again..." she said as she went to her section.   Once we were seated she came over smiling..."I see you're in my section after all..." she laughed.

"I'll start with the grilled sirloin steak with the house salad and baked potato – she'll have the meatloaf with macaroni & cheese, string beans, and carrots..." Bazil said as he continued looking at the menu...

"Okay! Will there be anything else?" she laughed.

"Yes – you just took our dinner order – now for breakfast, we'll each have your Uncle Herschel's Favorite."

"Hash brown casserole or fried apples?" the waitress asked.

"One with the hash brown casserole – one with fried apples – we'll share..." Bazil answered.

"Will that be ham, catfish, hamburger steak, chicken tenderloins, or pork chop?" the waitress asked.

"Hhmmmmm... Beautiee... you pick..." Bazil said.

"Catfish..." I answered.

"Very well – catfish it is – may I get some drinks for you?" the waitress asked.

"Coffee for me!" I said.

"Stewart's Root Beer for me..." Bazil said as he put the menus down.

"I'll be right back with your drinks..." the waitress said as she walked away...

"God you look good..." I breathed as I took Bazil's hand across the table...

"Do I feel as good as I look?" Bazil asked seductively as the waitress brought our drinks to the table...

"Yeeesss...." I breathed...

"Oh God – this is as good as crack!" Bazil said as he started drinking his soda..."

"Poor baby... I forgot you haven't had anything to eat or drink in months...

"Exactly..." Bazil said as the waitress brought our breakfast...

"Thank you..." I said as she put the plates down...

"I'll come back to check on you before bringing your other orders – this way you'll have room on the table – if that's alright..." the waitress said.

"That's fine..." Bazil said as he took my hands across the table... "Thank you God..." he whispered with tears in his eyes...

"Is he okay?" the waitress asked as she whipped tears out her eyes...

"He's fine..." I smiled.

"Okay – let's eat!" Bazil beamed as we started eating. "I missed you..." Bazil sighed as he talked to his food while eating it." I smiled as I watched him enjoy his food...

"How we 'doin over here?" the waitress asked when she came back to the table...

"Still hungry..." Bazil answered.

"I'll be right back..." she said as she went to get the rest of our food... "Will there be anything else?" she asked when she came back to the table with our plates...

"Check please..." Bazil said as he looked at me seductively. We finished eating without speaking, got up to leave, paid the check, and went out to the parking lot... "I can't wait for dessert..." Bazil whispered in my ear as he pulled me close to him...

"Neither can I..." I said as we got in the car and drove home.

Chapter 4

When we got to the house we sat in the car for a few minutes before getting out. "You ready my Thirst Quencher?"

"Ready..." he said as we got out the car and walked up to the front door...

"You okay?" I asked as I rubbed his back...

"Yea..." he said as he opened the door and we went inside... "C'mere..." he breathed as he pulled me into a kiss...

"Mmmmmm..." I moaned... "I missed you..."

"I missed you too... come with me..." he said as he pulled me into the living room... "Take off your clothes..." he commanded...

"Yes my Thirst Quencher..." I breathed as I stripped naked and stood in front of him...

"Sit on the couch... and spread your legs..."

"Yes my Thirst Quencher..." I breathed again. Bazil stripped out of his clothes and stood in front of me without speaking. I was dripping in anticipation of what was coming next. Bazil came up close, dropped to his knees, spread my legs, placed them up on his shoulders, and dove in... "Baaazzziiillll!!!" I screamed as he inserted two fingers in my pussy while licking and sucking. My legs trembled on his shoulders as he continued licking, sucking, and finger-fucking my pussy. I grabbed his head and rose up off the couch as he replaced his fingers with his tongue and I rode his face. Bazil continued to devour my pussy – so much so I could feel his teeth as he placed his hands under my ass, held me up, and sucked harder... "Ooohhh... Oooohhh... Oooohhh..." I moaned as I soaked his mouth, the couch, and his face... "Bazil... Bazil... Bazil... I'm cumming... I'm cumming... I'm cumming.... Aaaggghhhhh!" I collapsed on the couch to a degree but Bazil wouldn't let up – he held me up off the couch, spread my legs wider with his head, and sucked all my squirting... "Damn Bazil... Shit..." I breathed as he slowed down a bit but continued licking and sucking...

"Mmmmmm..." he moaned as my orgasm subsided... "Sweet..." he said as he stood up, got on top of me, and began thrusting inside me... standing back up...

"Oooohhhh...." I moaned as he started thrusting harder and deeper...

"Yeeesss.... Gimmie that pussy..." he growled...

"Fuck me Bazil..." I moaned. Bazil pushed me down on my back, climbed on top of me, and did as he was told...

"Is this what you want?" he growled as he fucked me harder...

"Bazzzziilll!" I screamed...

"Say it!" he growled...

"Fuck meeeeee!" I screamed as I came again...

"Uugghh! Uugghh! Uugghh! Uugghh! Uugghh!" Bazil collapsed on top of me and we both just lay there kissing... "I missed you Beautiee..."

"I missed you too..."

"I can tell..." he laughed as we continued kissing...

"Bazil..."

"Yes Beautiee..."

"Don't ever leave me again..."

"Never..."

"You promise?"

"Yeesss... I promise..."

"I love you my Thirst Quencher..."

"I love you too... let's go upstairs..." he said as he got up off me and picked up his clothes...

"Okay..." I said as he helped me up off the couch, picked up my clothes, and I followed him upstairs to our bedroom...

"Hmmmmm... this isn't the same room..." he said as he entered...

"I had it re-decorated..."

"Why?"

"I wanted it to look just like the hotel room where you proposed to me..." I answered as we sat on the bed...

"Aww..." he said as he pulled me into a kiss... "I need to ask you something Beautiee...

"Okay..."

"What happened?"

"You don't remember?"

"It's a bit fuzzy..."

"Tell me what you remember..."

"What happened Beautiee?"

"Tell me what you remember..."

"Beautiee..."

"Yes Bazil..."

"Tell me... please..."

"I need to know what you remember Bazil..." I pleaded with tears in my eyes...

"Don't cry Beautiee..." he said as he kissed me... I know it was bad... but I need to know..."

"Okay... let's get dressed..." I said as I tried to get my clothes...

"Let's not... tell me..."

"You were shot..."

"Where?"

"In here..."

"In this room?"

"Yes..."

"What happened?"

"I invited Sonia over... like you asked..."

"I asked you to invite Sonia over?"

"Yes..."

"Hmmmmm... why?"

"Because you wanted to watch us have sex..."

"Ohhh! So did she come over?"

"Yes..."

"Did you have sex?"

"Yes..."

"Was I watching?"

"Yes..."

"Where was I?"

"You were in the closet..."

"I was?"

"Yes..."

"Did I come out the closet?"

"Yes..."

"What happened after I came out the closet?"

"You joined us over there..." I said as I pointed to the area beneath the night stand...

"Did I participate?"

"Yes..."

"So... I was in the closet... I came out... I stood over there... and I was shot?"

"You came out the closet... you had sex with me while I was doing Sonia..."

"Oh... I see..."

"Then when Sonia started doing me... you came over here so you could put your dick in my mouth..."

"Oooohhh..."

"Trevor shot you..." I whispered. Bazil didn't say anything. He just sat there for a few minutes...

"You're lying..."

"No Bazil..."

"Trevor loves me... he would never hurt me..."

"Trevor shot you Bazil..."

"Are you sure?" he asked as he grabbed me by my shoulders...

"Bazil... you're scaring me..."

"Trevor was here? While we were having sex?"

"Yes..."

"And he shot me?"

"Yes..."

"Why?"

"Because you told him it was over between you..."

"Wait a minute... I'm starting to remember... you caught us together... you caught us... you left me... then you came back..."

"That's right..."

"How did Trevor get in here?"

"Sonia set us up..."

"Sonia?"

"Yes..."

"Are you sure?"

"Yes..."

"How do you know?"

"I saw the gun..." I answered as I started to cry... "I yelled for you to look out but you didn't move fast enough... and he shot you..."

"Beautiee... it's okay... I'm here..." Bazil said as he held me...

"No it isn't!" I yelled... "He tried to kill me too!"

"What did you say?"

"After he shot you... he pointed the gun at me... I pulled Sonia down on top of me... but

Sonia got hit... he dropped the gun and came over to Sonia... he told me it was all my fault... he said Sonia didn't deserve to die..." I cried...

"Sonia? Sonia and Trevor?"

"I picked up the gun... I told him she deserved to die and so did he... and I shot him..." I cried...

"I'm so sorry... please don't cry..." Bazil said as he started crying too...

"Katina arrested me..."

"What?!"

"I was charged with attempted murder, murder, and murder!"

"Beautiee... Nooooo....."

"My bail was set at $200,000! I put up my house to make bail!"

"Why Trevor Why?" Bazil cried as he continued to hold me and we cried together...

"Because you chose me Bazil..."

"Damn right I chose you... I love you sooo much... you went through this all alone..."

"I wasn't alone..."

"You weren't alone?"

"Keisha and Troy were here when the paramedics came..." I said as I started crying again... "Keisha rode with me to the hospital... she never left my side..."

"I'm sorry..." Bazil said, crying as he held me...

"When Trevor shot you I screamed... Keisha told Troy to break the door down... they both came running upstairs... they saw us naked... I was covered in blood... you were lying on the floor over there... Sonia was on the bed... Trevor was over there..."

"I'm sorry... I'm sorry..."

"They stayed with me at the hospital... they took me to eat... they even paid to have the house cleaned so when I came home it looked as if nothing happened – I don't know what I would have done without them..."

"I'm sorry..."

"I was naked, covered in blood – they swabbed me to get samples – they even wanted to do a rape kit!"

"Oh my God... No... Please tell me..."

"Trevor didn't rape me... he never touched me...

"Oh thank God..."

"I went to work to let everyone know what happened... Samuel has been Acting President in your absence..."

"I love you soooo much... you went through all this... you never left me... you held me down..." Bazil said as he broke down crying...

"Smalls held us both down..."

"Smalls?"

"Yea..." Bazil stopped crying and started to smile.

"I owe him my life... he held you down... let's get dressed..." Bazil said as he started getting dressed...

"I thought you didn't want to?"

"I didn't... but I need to go see Smalls..."

"Can't you go later... please?" I pleaded as I looked up at him... tugging on his pants to bring him closer to me...

"I guess I can go see him later..." he said as I loosened his pants, dropped them to the floor along with his boxers, and pulled him closer to my mouth... "Beautiee..." he moaned as I began sucking his dick. I grabbed his ass and pushed him deeper into my mouth as he grabbed my head. I relaxed my throat as he closed his eyes, leaned his head back, and fucked my mouth...

"Mmmmmm..." I moaned so he could feel the vibration...

"Shiiittt... that's it... take this dick... suck it..." I began alternating between pulling his dick all the way out my mouth and deep throating him as he watched...

"I missed you my Thirst Quencher..." I said as I pulled his dick out my mouth and deep throated him again...

"I can tell..." Bazil breathed, smiling as he watched me enjoy pleasing him...

"Cum in my mouth..." I commanded...

"Oh shit... fuck... that's it... suck it... suck it... Ugghh! Ugghh! Ugghh!" I swallowed every bit and continued sucking as Bazil started shaking... "Easy Beautiee... I'm a bit sensitive..."

"Mmmmm..." I moaned as I continued sucking a little softer...

"You want more?" he breathed...

"Yes... I want more..."

"Gimmie a minute... I need to re-energize... I'm a little weak... you sucked the shit outta me..."

"I couldn't help it..." I said as I continued sucking his dick softly...

"Let's get in bed..."

"Okay..." I said as I moved back on the bed and pulled him down on top of me...

"I love you..." Bazil said as he kissed me...

"I love you too..."

"I need some sleep..." he yawned as he lay beside me...

"So do I..." I yawned as I snuggled underneath him and we fell asleep.

Chapter 5

"Smalls – how may I help you?" he greeted as he answered his cell.

"It's Bazil..."

"What now Bazil?"

"You don't sound like you're happy to hear from me..."

"I'm not..."

"Would you have been happier if I died?"

"Of course not..."

"So you are happy to hear from me then..."

"I'm happy Trevor didn't kill you or Beautiee..."

"Thank you..."

"Don't thank me Bazil..."

"Why not?"

"Because I didn't do it for you... I did it for her..."

"I know..."

"She should have never been in that situation! She could've been killed!"

"I know..."

"What if you died Bazil? Where would that have left her? Did you ever stop to think about that Bazil?"

"No..."

"I can't help you anymore Bazil..."

"Nonsense..."

"I'm serious... Katina's been asking a lot of questions..."

"What questions?"

"She's looking into the disappearance of Billie..."

"Who's Billie?"

"Cut the shit – you know damn well who Billie is... and so does Katina..."

"So what?"

"So is she going to find anything?"

"I have no idea..."

"See? This that bullshit – I'm not helping you this time..."

"Smalls..."

"What?"

"We're going to continue to help each other..."

"I'm not going down for this shit Bazil!"

"Smalls... have I ever put you in harm's way?"

"No..."

"Okay then... and I'm not about to..."

"There's more..."

"What is it Smalls?"

"Katina's been looking into the disappearance of MaryJane LaRue too..."

"Is MaryJane missing?"

"Bazil..."

"Yes Smalls?"

"I helped myself to a larger retainer while you were sleeping..."

"How much larger?"

"$100k..."

"Whatever you need is fine..."

"Bring Beautiee to see me... I need to speak to you both...

"Okay... we'll be there later today..."

"See you later..." Smalls said as he hung up. "Good morning... we both need to get dressed..." Bazil said as he kissed me awake...

"Come back to bed..." I moaned...

"We need to go see Smalls..." Bazil said as he climbed on top of me...

"I need to eat..." I moaned as we started kissing...

"Are you hungry?" Bazil asked as he thrust himself inside me...

"Yeesss... I'm hungry!" I moaned as Bazil thrust harder and deeper...

"I'm a bit hungry myself..." Bazil breathed in my ear before he started kissing my neck...

"Bazil..." I moaned as I spread my legs, grabbed his ass, and pushed him in deeper....

"Mmmmm..." Bazil moaned into my mouth as he kissed me fully....

"Mmmmm... Mmmmm... Mmmmm..." I moaned back into his mouth as I was cumming...

"Mmmmmph! Mmmmmph! Mmmmmph!" Bazil moaned into my mouth before collapsing down on top of me. We continued kissing for a few moments until Bazil spoke... "We need to get dressed..." he said between kisses...

"No..." I breathed as he tried to get up and I pulled him back down on top of me...

"Beautiee..."

"Yes my Thirst Quencher..."

"We need to go see Smalls..."

"Please... Don't make me go..." I pleaded as we continued kissing...

"Beautiee..."

"No..." I whispered as I started to cry...

"Beautiee..." Bazil whispered as he kissed my tears...

"I just want this to be over..."

"I know..."

"I'm tired Bazil..."

"I know... I'm sorry..." Bazil whispered as he started to cry...

"Don't cry Bazil..." I whispered as I kissed his tears and his lips...

"I love you so much Beautiee..." he whispered as he continued crying...

"I love you too... please don't cry..."

"I'll stop if you stop..."

"Okay... I'll go see Smalls..."

"Okay... let's get dressed before you change your mind..."

"Mmmmm... you keep kissing me like this and we're not going anywhere..." I breathed as I rolled him over and slid down between his legs...

"Beautiee... No..."

"Wait a minute..." I laughed... "Did you just say no to me?"

"I guess I did..." he laughed...

"Remember that..." I laughed as I jumped up, ran to the bathroom, and jumped in the shower...

"Where do you think you're going?" Bazil laughed as he turned me around and pulled me into a kiss...

"To... see... Smalls..." I moaned as he put his hand between my legs...

"I'm sorry I told you no..." he breathed as I started playing with his dick...

"Apology not accepted!" I laughed as I threw the loofah full of soap at him...

"Oh... okay... it's like that is it?" he laughed as he grabbed me, shoved me into the corner, and held me against the wall with his body... "Please... accept... my... apology..." he breathed between kisses...

"No... I won't..." I laughed.

"Okay..." he relented as he pushed me down on the bench and brought his dick to my mouth...

"My... Thirst... Quencher..." I moaned as I put his dick in my mouth and began sucking it...

"Yesss..."

"Don't... you... ever... tell... me... no... again..." I breathed as I sucked his dick... "Do... you... understand... me... my... Thirst... Quencher?"

"Yeeesss..." Bazil moaned...

"Who's... dick... is... this?"

"Yoouuurrrsss..."

"That's... right... now... give... it... to... me..."

"Oh shit... fuck... Aggghhh!"

"Mmmmm..." I moaned as I continued sucking Bazil's dick until his orgasm subsided...

"Damn..." he breathed as he pulled me up from the bench, pulled me close to him, and kissed me hard. I grabbed the loofah with one hand, soaped it up with the other, and washed the back of Bazil's body as he held me. Bazil loosened his grip a little as I washed the front of his body, never letting go of me. When I was done he took the loofah as I held onto him, soaped it up, and pulled me into a kiss as he washed the back of my body. I loosened my grip a little as he started washing the front of my body...

"Oh Bazil..." I moaned as he began kissing my neck, then sucking my breasts as he washed them... "Bazil..." I moaned as he began washing my pussy, swirling the loofah around my clit... "Mmmmm... Mmmmm...." I moaned as Bazil dropped the loofah and began fucking me with his fingers...

"Now I'm thirsty..." Bazil growled as he sat on the bench and dove between my legs...

"Bazil... Bazil... Bazil..." I moaned as he licked and sucked my pussy while finger-fucking me...

"Mmmmm... he moaned as I started cumming and my legs started shaking...

"Bazil! I'm cumming! I'm cumming!" Bazil slowed down but continued to lick, suck, and fuck me with his fingers as my orgasm subsided. When he was finished he stood up, pulled me into a kiss, and whispered in my ear...

"Do you accept my apology now?"

"Yes my Thirst Quencher..." I breathed... "Yeeessss..."

Chapter 6

"Well it's about Damn time!" Smalls laughed as he grabbed Bazil into a hug.

"I love you brother..." Bazil said as he kissed Smalls in the mouth...

"I love you too man..." Smalls said as they embraced for a moment...

"Ahem?" I exclaimed to get their attention...

"Beautiee!" Smalls said as he grabbed me into a hug and tried to kiss me...

"Oh no – don't act like you love me now!" I laughed as I pushed him away...

"C'mere you!" he said, grabbing me into a kiss before I could object...

"Watch it!" Bazil laughed.

"Sit down y'all – we have a lot to go over..." Smalls said as he got serious...

"What's going on Smalls?" Bazil asked...

"Let's start with Beautiee..."

"Okay..." I sighed...

"Beautiee – we got a hold of the surveillance footage..."

"Surveillance?" Bazil asked...

"Bazil... be quiet... this isn't about you... yet..." Smalls said...

"Go 'head man..." Bazil said...

"Beautiee – we got a hold of the surveillance..."

"That's good..." I said...

"Not really..."

"Why not?"

"It shows Trevor just opened the door and walked right in – Katina's going to present it to the D.A. as if he was invited..."

"He wasn't fucking invited!" Bazil growled.

"I know that Bazil – but this is about Beautiee... please..."

"I didn't invite him..." I said as I started to cry...

"I swear to God – if that mutha fucka wasn't already dead I'd fuckin' kill him!" Bazil yelled.

"Damnit Bazil – shut the fuck up!" Smalls yelled.

"Do you know who the fuck you're talking to?" Bazil growled.

"I'm talking to Bazil J. Osgood – known felon – convicted murder – person of interest in the disappearance of Beautiee's ex-husband, Billie and also person of interest in the disappearance of your former employee, MaryJane LaRue – but I'm also talking to my brother and my friend – now shut the fuck up! Please!"

"I'm sorry..." Bazil sighed.

"Beautiee – as long as you tell me you didn't invite him that's what I'll present to the D.A. – but I have to be honest – Beverly is going to try to convince the judge that you didn't kill him in self-defense – you killed him because you were jealous of his relationship with Bazil..."

"I should've killed that mutha-fucka when I had the chance..." I mumbled...

"What did you just say?" Smalls asked.

"I said I killed him in self-defense..."

"That's what I thought you said..." Smalls reiterated...

"Are you telling us my wife can be convicted?" Bazil asked...

"Beverly will send it to the Grand Jury – it's circumstantial – but..."

"But what Smalls?"

"It's you Bazil..." Smalls sighed...

"Beautiee... I'm sorry..." Bazil whispered as tears streamed down his face...

"Don't cry Bazil..." I said as I took his hand and cried with him. Smalls handed us a box of tissues after taking some for himself...

"I wish I never knew Trevor..." Bazil cried...

"I wish you never knew him either..." I cried...

"Beautiee... I need to ask you something..." Smalls said...

"Yes?"

"What happened to your ex-husband?"

"I have no idea..."

"Beautiee... they have the surveillance..."

"What surveillance?"

"They have the surveillance from the hotel..." Bazil answered.

"Is that true?" I cried.

"Yes Beautiee..." Smalls answered.

"Why?"

"Katina has a bug up her ass when it comes to Bazil – they've been watching him ever since he got out of prison..." Smalls explained.

"Beautiee had nothing to do with that..." Bazil said...

"Don't say another fuckin' word Bazil..." Smalls growled...

"I said Beautiee had nothing to do with that..." Bazil repeated...

"What are you telling me Bazil?" Smalls asked...

"I'm not telling you anything..."

"Are they going to find anything Bazil?"

"There's nothing to find..."

"Bazil... you know you can tell me anything... right?"

"Yes Smalls..."

"You know our conversations are privileged right?"

"Yes Smalls..."

"Okay... as your attorney... I'm asking you... is there anything you need to tell me?"

"Yes..."

"Damn... I knew it... go 'head..."

"Billie was in prison with us..."

"You... and Trevor?"

"Yes..."

"Okay – good – continue..."

"I never trusted that mutha fucka... but he was very close to Trevor..."

"How close?"

"One night I heard Trevor screaming for help... Billie owed a debt... and he was trying to pay that debt with Trevor..." Bazil said as he started tearing up...

"You loved him... didn't you?"

"Yes..."

"Damn... I hope this doesn't come out in court... but it probably will..."

"There's more..."

"What else?" Smalls asked as he threw up his hands...

"Billie told Trevor all about Beautiee..."

"So what?"

"So he told Trevor that he was going to get revenge on her for leaving him as soon as he got out of prison..."

"So that's what happened at the hotel?"

"Yes..."

"Damn... so you knew who Beautiee was all along..."

"No..."

"You didn't know who Beautiee was?"

"I met Beautiee that night at the hotel... and I fell in love with her..." Bazil said as he took my hand...

"Hmmmmm... this is hearsay... but it might help..."

"How?" I asked...

"Maybe Trevor wanted to get revenge on Billie... for what happened in prison..."

"Maybe..." Bazil smiled...

"And maybe... Trevor wanted Bazil out of the way... so he could have Beautiee all to himself..."

"Maybe..." Bazil smiled again...

"I can't prove it... but they can't either..." Smalls smiled... "Thank you for telling me Bazil..."

"You're welcome..." Bazil smiled...

"Bazil... there's something you need to do..."

"What's that?"

"You need to tell Beautiee the truth..."

"What's he talking about Bazil?" I asked with tears in my eyes...

"I can't..." Bazil whispered...

"Bazil... please..." I whispered...

"I'm scared..." Bazil whispered as he cried...

"Don't cry Bazil..." I said as I kissed his tears...

"Please don't leave me Beautiee..." he cried...

"Never..." I said as I pulled him into a kiss...

"Promise?"

"Promise..."

"I killed her..."

"Who?"

"Janet..."

"Who's Janet?"

"My first wife..."

"Why Bazil?"

"Because she tried to leave me..."

"Like me?"

"Yes..."

"So... that night... we're you going to kill me too Bazil?"

"No Beautiee..."

"The only reason I got away from you is because I shot you..."

"What?!" Smalls interrupted...

"Beautiee... I didn't mean to kill Janet... it was an accident..."

"Like me?"

"She hit her head on the counter... I begged her not to leave me..."

"So that night... when you threw me into the counter... and I stabbed you... what were you planning to do to me Bazil? Huh?"

"I wasn't planning to kill you... I swear..."

"What if I didn't have the gun? What if I couldn't defend myself? Would I be dead right now?" I yelled...

"No Beautiee..." Bazil cried...

"How can I be sure?" I whispered with tears in my eyes...

"I wasn't trying to kill you Beautiee... I swear... please believe me..." he said as he broke down crying...

"What were you planning to do Bazil?" I asked with tears in my eyes...

"I was planning to lock you up in the house until I could convince you to stay..." Bazil cried as he dropped to his knees and held me by my legs...

"Okay..."

"So you believe me?" Bazil asked as he got up and sat beside me...

"Yes Bazil... I believe you..."

"I love you so much..."

"I love you too..."

"Hold up!" Smalls interrupted...

"Yes?" I answered.

"You shot Bazil?"

"Yea..."

"When?"

"When Katina came to the house..."

"Oh Shit! Does she know that?"

"She thinks Bazil was hurting me – she gave me her card and warned me my husband was a dangerous man..." I laughed.

"Did anyone hear gun shots?"

"It was only one shot – and I told Katina we were watching Law & Order..."

"Wait – I can't wich' y'all!' Smalls laughed.

"I need to tell you something..." I said.

"Yes Beautiee?" Smalls asked...

"I'm the one responsible for the disappearance of MaryJane LaRue…

"Oh shit! Y'all some gangstas! Le'me write this shit down!" Smalls said as he grabbed a pad and started scribbling…

"I went to see Bazil at work…"

"Uh huh…" Smalls said as he kept scribbling…"

"I walked into Bazil's office…"

"Uh huh…"

"And I caught him fuckin' the Bitch!"

"What?! Damn Bazil! What the fuck is wrong with you?" Smalls yelled. Bazil didn't say anything… he just went along with my story…

"Bazil jumped up when he saw me…"

"Uh huh…" Smalls said as he kept scribbling…

"And I went over to her, snatched her up by her fuckin' hair, dragged her ass to the door, and bounced her out on her ass! Right Bazil?"

"Yea…" Bazil acknowledged…

"Uh huh…" Smalls said, still scribbling…

"I told her she was fired – and I also told her if I ever caught her near my husband again I would fuckin' kill her! Isn't that right Bazil?"

"Yea…" Bazil acknowledged…

"Where's the gun?" Smalls asked…

"What gun?" I asked…

"The gun you shot Bazil with?"

"It doesn't exist…" I answered…

"So… to be clear… you caught your husband cheating on you with her – you told her she was fired – and you threatened to kill her if you ever saw her near your husband again?" Smalls asked.

"That's right..." I answered...

"Where there witnesses?" Smalls asked...

"Joselyn Logan..."

"Who's she?"

"Bazil's new Personal Assistant."

"She witnessed this?"

"Yes..."

"And she heard you threaten MaryJane LaRue?"

"Yes..."

"That might be a problem..."

"For who?"

"For you – she'll be called to testify..."

"So what?"

"Beautiee – you just admitted you threatened her..."

"Yes I did – and there isn't a woman anywhere in the world – including the D.A. – that will blame me or convict me for threatening to kill the woman I caught fucking my husband!" I said matter-of-factly.

"Hmmmmmm... you're probably right... so... just to be clear... Bazil – you had nothing to do with the disappearance of MaryJane LaRue?"

"No... I didn't..." Bazil answered...

"And... to be clear... you haven't seen her - or been with her since she was fired?"

"Hell no!" Bazil answered...

"Okay – this is good – I'll keep you posted – Beautiee – could you give us some privacy?" Smalls asked.

"Uummmmm... okay..." I hesitated as I got up to go sit outside in the waiting area.

"Help yourself to coffee... or anything else you want..." he said as I opened the door to leave...

"Okay – thanks..." I said as I closed the door. "I guess they want to catch up..." I said out loud as I made myself some coffee, sat down on the sofa, and made myself comfortable...

"Bazil J. Osgood – you owe me one million dollars!" Smalls laughed.

"You already helped yourself to an additional 100k – how much more do you want?" Bazil laughed...

"My brother – you made me a bet – and I'm cashing in my chip!" Smalls laughed.

"Damn... I forgot..."

"I didn't!"

"I'm a man of my word..." Bazil sighed...

"It's cool – you're my best client – and now your wife is also my client – I know I'll never be broke – I'll just help myself to additional retainers... as I need them..." Smalls laughed.

"You're enjoying this aren't you?"

"Hell yea! I told you one day you're gonna meet the right woman – and Beautiee is that woman!" he laughed.

"Yes she is – go 'head... let me have it..."

"Oh I'm just getting started!" Smalls laughed.

"I need a drink for this..." Bazil sighed...

"Here you go!" Smalls laughed as he pulled out a bottle of Jack Daniels, pulled out two glasses, and poured two drinks... "Here's to Beautiee..." he said as he raised his glass...

"To Beautiee..." Bazil repeated as he shook his head...

"The woman who successfully pussy-whipped your ass!" Smalls laughed as he drank... "Drink up muthafucka!" Smalls laughed...

"The woman who successfully pussy-whipped my ass... damn!" Bazil laughed as he drank and put the glass on the table...

"Oh we're not done!" Smalls laughed as he poured them both another...

"Go 'head..." Bazil laughed... "I know I had this coming..." he said before slurping down his drink...

"Hell yea you had this coming!" Smalls laughed as he gulped down his drink... "Put it here!" Smalls laughed as he banged on the table...

"Alright... alright..." Bazil laughed as he put the glass on the table and Smalls poured them another drink...

"You got caught fuckin' another woman – she's still here!" he laughed as they gulped another drink down. Bazil didn't bother objecting... he just put the glass down on the table and waited for the next one... "You got caught fuckin' another man – in your house – she's still here!" Smalls laughed as Bazil waited for the next drink... "You had a fight... she stabbed you... shot you... left you... and came back!" Smalls laughed as he waited for Bazil to put the glass back on the table so he could pour some more... "The man you fought over tried to kill you – and her – and she still ain't leave your ass!" Smalls laughed as Bazil finished his drink and held the glass in his hand... "Don't stop now muthafucka!" he laughed as he pointed to the table. Bazil put the glass on the table and watched as Smalls poured another drink for them... "The woman who held you down while you were in a comma!" he laughed as they drank. Bazil put the glass on the tip of the table – nearly dropping it... "The woman who went to jail for you!" Smalls laughed as he poured another drink for them... "The woman who put up her house for you!" Smalls was laughing uncontrollably at this point, spilling some liquor as he poured more drinks... "The woman who... I just watched you beg not to leave... even after she found out you killed your first wife!" Smalls continued to laugh and continued to pour...

"The woman who asked God for me..." Bazil slurred as they drank...

"What did you say?" Smalls asked, wide-eyed.

"When I went into a comma I died... and Beautiee came to get me..." Bazil whispered...

"Are you drunk Bazil?" Smalls asked...

"Drunk... and serious..."

"You died?"

"Yes... and Beautiee died with me... I told her she needed to go back... but she said she couldn't live without me..." he cried...

"Damn Bazil..." Smalls said as he started crying too...

"We saw God... God told Beautiee to trust him and he sent her back... I begged God not to let Beautiee live without me... and he gave me another chance..." Bazil said as he broke down...

"Here's to the woman that asked God for you..." Smalls said with tears as they both finished the bottle of Jack Daniels...

"To the woman that asked God... for me... for me..." Bazil cried...

"Damn... where can I find a woman like that?" Smalls asked.

"Ask God for her..." Bazil answered as he fell back in the chair... and they both started snoring in their drunken stupor...

"Guys?" I said as I knocked on the office door... "Hello?" I said as I opened the door and went inside... "Bazil..." I whispered as I tried to wake him... and then I saw the empty bottle of Jack Daniels and the two empty glasses... "Well damn!" I laughed... "What the hell were you celebrating?" I said out loud as I picked up the empty bottle of Jack Daniels, put it in the trash, and put the empty glasses on the table... "Oh shoot... is that Bazil's phone?" I asked out loud as I looked around... "Oh shoot – that's Small's phone!" I said as I took it out of his pocket and answered it... "Attorney Smalls office – may I help you?"

"This is Katina – is Smalls available?"

"He's out right now – may I have him return your call?"

"Yes please..."

"May I tell him what it's in reference to?"

"Tell him Beautiee Osgood – urgent."

"I sure will..." I said as I hung up...

"Beautiee..." Bazil yawned as he tried to sit up... "Oh damn – my head hurts – I'm gonna be sick!" Bazil yelled as he stumbled to the toilet just in time... "Uuuggghhh!" I heard as everything came up and into the toilet...

"Damn... what's that smell?" Smalls said as he woke up... "Oh shit – move Bazil!" he yelled as he hit the toilet just in time... "Oh God – I'm gonna die!" he moaned...

"Serves your ass right!" Bazil laughed. I watched them both in the bathroom as Bazil used the mouthwash and then Smalls.

"Next time we'll go out to eat – then we'll drink!" Smalls sighed...

"There won't be a next time!" Bazil laughed...

"Hey Beautiee... you alright?" Smalls asked...

"I'm fine," I laughed...

"Shit – where's my phone..."

"Here..." I said as I handed him his phone...

"Oh shit – Katina called..."

"I know..."

"You answered my phone?"

"Yes..."

"What she say?"

"She said please call her regarding Beautiee Osgood – urgent..."

"Damn – that's not good – I gotta go – I'll call you!" Smalls yelled as he ran out the office...

"C'mon Bazil..." I sighed as I opened the door to Smalls' office so we could leave...

"We need to get down to the station..." Bazil said...

"No we don't!" I yelled

"Smalls said..."

"I heard what Smalls said! I'm going home – with you – end of discussion!"

"Okay Beautiee..." Bazil said as he kissed me... "Whatever you want..."

"Right now I want you..."

"That's fine with me..." Bazil said as he kissed me again.

Chapter 7

"Hey Smalls," Bazil smiled as he opened the door to let Smalls inside...

"It's not good..." Smalls said as he came inside and closed the door behind him...

"What's wrong?" Bazil asked as he pulled me close to him...

"We need to sit down..." Smalls said as we followed him into the living room. Smalls sat on the chair, we sat on the sofa, and then Smalls continued... "The Grand Jury found probable cause... they've issued an indictment...

"Don't worry Beautiee... I gotchu..." Bazil said as I started crying...

"There's more..." Smalls sighed...

"What's wrong?" Bazil asked...

"Beverly filed a motion to revoke bond... and the judge granted the motion..."

"Whhhyyyyy?" I cried...

"Because of me..." Bazil answered with tears in his eyes...

"Because you're charged with a double homicide and the attempted murder of your husband, the prosecutor believes you'll run..." Smalls continued...

"I'm not going anywhere!" I screamed...

"They know that – they just want to break you!" Smalls gritted as he slammed his fist on the end table...

"So I'm going back to jail..." I whispered...

"Yes Beautiee..." Bazil answered...

"For how long?" I asked.

"You'll be in jail until you go to trial... and during the trial..." Smalls sighed...

"This isn't right..." I cried...

"Bazil?"

"Yes Smalls?"

"Promise me you won't do anything stupid..."

"Get the fuck out..." Bazil said as he stood up...

"I'm sorry..." Smalls said as he stood up to leave...

"Wait a minute!" I yelled.

"Yes Beautiee?" Smalls asked as he turned to face me...

"What the fuck am I supposed to do now? Wait for them to knock on the door? Wait for them to arrest me at work? How much time do we have?" Smalls didn't answer right away. He just stood there looking at us for a few moments before Bazil spoke...

"She has to turn herself in doesn't she?"

"I'm afraid so..." Smalls answered with his head down...

"When?" I asked...

"Tomorrow morning..." Smalls answered as he headed towards the front door...

"Will you be there?" I asked as he opened the door to leave...

"I'll see you in the morning," Smalls answered as he closed the door behind him...

"Come here Beautiee..." Bazil said as he pulled me into a kiss... "Please don't cry..." he said as he began kissing my tears off my face to no avail...

"Hey Smalls..." Bazil said as he opened the door..."

"Hey Bazil..." Smalls sighed. "You ready Beautiee?"

"No..." I whispered as tears streamed down my face...

"Please don't go..." Bazil cried as he grabbed me and held on tight...

"I don't want to..." I cried..."but I have to..."

"You don't have to..." Bazil cried as he kissed me... "We can run... we can go anywhere you want... just don't leave me... please..."

"I want to..." I cried between kisses... "but I can't..."

"You promised me... you'd never leave me again..."

"I know... I'm sorry... my Thirst Quencher..." At this point, Smalls was crying too. In that moment – I wanted to run. I didn't want to leave his arms. I wanted Bazil to take me away from all of it... but I knew I couldn't do that either... "I'll make it up to you... when I come back..."

"You promise?"

"Yes... my Thirst Quencher... I promise..." Bazil let me go, but he continued crying as I walked over to Smalls...

"Let's go..." Smalls said with tears in his eyes. I opened the door without looking back because I knew if I did — I wouldn't go through with it. Smalls and I walked out the door and when Bazil closed the door behind us, he broke down crying hard. I started to turn around and run back to Bazil, but Smalls put his hand on my shoulder. We stood in the driveway for a few moments until I gathered myself, Smalls wiped his tears, we got in the car, and headed to the Bridgeport Correctional Center.

Chapter 8

"How many we got today?" She asked as Smalls took me inside...

"Ten..." somebody answered.

"Name?" she asked when I got to the window...

"Beautiee Osgood..." Smalls answered.

"Are you her attorney?"

"Yes I am."

"Fill out this form please – Beautiee – come with me..." she said as she came out from behind the window. I ran to Smalls and threw my arms around him...

"I know..." he whispered as he hugged me back... "I'll be back as soon as I can..." Smalls said as he let me go and I watched him leave...

"Let me give you a piece of advice – suck up those damn tears – weak Bitches don't make it in here," she said as she pulled me behind the door with the other inmates...

"Let me tell you something..." I said. She stopped abruptly, turned to face me, put her hands on her hips, and looked me up and down before she asked... "What – little girl?"

"I'm nobody's weak Bitch..." I said with a smile.

"Ooohhh... it's like that... okay... we'll see..." she laughed as she turned back around and I followed her to the back of the line with the other inmates... "Attention Ladies..." she said as she walked from the beginning of the line to the end of the line and back to the beginning... "My name is Gert – I'll be processing each of you. You'll take off your clothes, you'll squat, you'll cough, and then you'll be escorted to the shower. After you take a shower, you'll put on this jumpsuit and you'll be brought back here. You'll each receive an Inmate ID, an Inmate Number, and an Inmate Handbook – I suggest you take the time to read the manual so you know what's expected of you. We'll begin shortly..." she said as she walked away to speak to someone else... "That one at the end talkin' about she's nobody's weak Bitch – we'll see if she talks that same shit after she meets Ugly..." she laughed.

"Girl – you don't know who that is?"

"Should I?"

"That's Beautiee Osgood!"

"Yea – so what?"

"That's Bazil's wife!"

"Oh shit! The one that was charged with the attempted murder plus two other murders? That's her?"

"Yea – that's her!"

"Damn Veronica – why didn't you tell me?"

"I thought you knew — everybody else knows!"

"Shit — if she's in her for all that — Ugly might be in trouble..." she laughed as she headed back to the line... "Alright ladies — one at a time — don't be shy — we all got the same thing — does anybody need pads?"

"I do..." Someone said...

"Me too..." someone else said...

"Me too!" I said quickly. I didn't really need a pad — I just wanted to get off the line like the other ladies...

"Come with me y'all — Veronica — can you get them while I process these ladies?"

"Okay..." she said as she went to the line...

"This way ladies..." Gert said and we all followed. We were all escorted to a waiting room. I watched as the first inmate left and then the second. "Alright Beautiee — your turn... "Gert said as she took me to a room with a private shower... "Take off your clothes — put them in this bag — and put this pad on..." she said as she gave me the pad...

"Thanks — I don't need it..." I said as I stripped and put my things in the plastic bag..."

"You could'a stayed on the line with the other ladies..." she said as she pulled me towards the shower...

"I could've... but I didn't want to..." I smiled.

"This isn't a game..." Gert said, annoyed...

"Good – 'cause if this was a game – I'd forfeit..." I said.

"Squat and cough." I did as I was told and stood up. "Take a shower and put on this jumpsuit..." she said as she handed me the jumpsuit. I took the quickest shower I've ever taken, dried off, and put on the jumpsuit. "C'mon..." she said as she took me by the arm and escorted me back to where the other ladies were being processed. "Here's your Inmate ID, your Inmate Number, and your Inmate Handbook – read it or not – time to go to your cell..." she said as she took me by the arm again and brought me to my cell. On the way down, I saw other ladies in their cells. Some looked up at me, some didn't pay me any mind – but one in particular stared right through me...

"Oh great – just what I need – please leave me alone..." I sighed to myself as I waked past her...

"Here's your cell – the doors stay open for a while – the common area's over there – they'll be an announcement when it's light out – once they make that announcement, everyone is to return to their cell for the night – welcome to prison..." she said as she turned and walked off.

"Sigh... I might as well sit down and get comfortable..." I said as I sat on the hard bed, picked up the Inmate Handbook, and started reading...

"Why you bein' all anti-social?" she asked as she came into my cell..."

"Oh God... I knew it..." I thought to myself before I spoke... "I'm just tired... it's been that kinda day..."

"You have plenty of time to read that damn book – let's go..." she said as she tried to grab me..."

"Don't touch me!" I snapped as I pulled my arm away...

"I'll touch you if I want to... when I want to..." she said as she walked towards me, backing me into a corner. By this time, all the other inmates gathered outside my cell to watch what was about to go down...

"I said don't touch me..."

"Why not? Don't you like girls?" she said as she touched my cheek...

"Stop it!" I yelled as I pushed her into the wall...

"This is gonna be fun..." she said as she came towards me and tried to kiss me..."

"Oh hell no!" I yelled as I lunged at her, knocking her to the floor. I jumped down and commenced to stomping that ass... "Don't – you – ever – touch – me – again – with – your – Burly - lookin' – ass – do – you – understand – me?" I got up and stood there with my fists clenched, ready to beat her ass down if she tried to come at me again...

"Alright – damn!" she laughed as she got up off the floor and wiped the blood off her mouth...

"Hmmm... I guess she ain't nobody's weak Bitch..." Gert laughed to herself as she watched from the other side before she came over... "Okay – shows over – clear out..." Gert said as she shooed everyone away from my cell.

"Now...where was I..." I sighed as I picked up the Inmate Handbook and started reading. The first thing I noticed was the handbook was 42 pages. "Damn..." I said out loud... "Oh well – at least I won't be bored..." I said out loud as I read the mission statement:

The Bridgeport Correctional Center shall protect the public, protect staff and provide safe, secure and humane supervision of offenders with opportunities that support restitution and rehabilitation by providing meaningful programming designed to support successful community re-integration.

"Bullshit!" I flipped to the table of contents and scrolled down to Addressing Staff, Following Orders, Personal Conduct, and Personal Safety – page 6... "More Bullshit!" I said as I continued reading – especially when I got to Personal Conduct:

You are required to conduct yourself in a responsible manner. A. You are not permitted to engage in behavior that disrupts the order of the facility, threatens security, endangers the safety of any person or imperils state or personal property. B. You are not permitted to make sexually suggestive remarks or gestures to any person. C. You are not permitted to make excessive noise or to use profanity. "So what the fuck just happened to me then?" I shook my head and started reading the paragraph under Personal Safety:

If you believe that your safety is at risk, report your concerns to a staff member immediately. The Department of Correction and this facility are committed to ensuring your safety.

"Yea right – fuckin' staff stood right there and watched – only thing they were committed to was declaring a winner in the fight!" I snapped. I glanced at the Clothing/Accessory, Personal Hygiene, Housing Unit rules, Fire Safety, Movement and Corridor Regulations and stopped to read what was outlined under Dining Hall:

1. You will have five (5) minutes after chow call to leave the unit before you are late. Being late will cause you to miss chow.
2. Cutting in line is not permitted.
3. You are responsible for receiving a complete tray; only one (1) trip through the serving line is allowed.
4. You are required to sit in the seat next to the last occupied seat at each table. Skipping seats is not permitted.

5. No items may be taken into the dining hall except your own utensils; no items may be taken from the dining hall.

6. You must eat with your housing unit or work detail.

7. You will have twenty (20) minutes to eat your meal.

8. You must take your tray to the scullery after you finish your meal and scrape it into the proper container provided.

9. You must leave the dining hall after you finish eating and proceed to your housing unit or assigned area.

I started crying when I got to page 22 and read paragraph A. under the Mail Section:

You may correspond and receive an unlimited number of correspondence at your own expense. You may write to anyone except: a victim of any crime you have been convicted of or in which disposition is pending...

"Oh Bazil..." I cried. When I got to page 25 and read the paragraph under Initial Visit it made me feel even worse:

You may receive two (2) adult visitors from your immediate family pending completion of processing your visiting Application Form or for seventy-two (72) hours after admission. You may add your two immediate family members to your visiting list after intake by submitting a request to your counselor. A back ground check will be conducted and they must have the same last name as you.

"I can't even have visitors..." I cried. "Everyone in my immediate family is married – no one has the same name as me." I didn't feel any better reading the Immediate Family or the Expanded Family Section either – I couldn't see my husband, my parents lived down south, and we don't have children. I kept turning the pages until I turned to page 27 and read the paragraph under Section G. Privileged and Professional Visits:

Visits between an inmate and their attorney or other credential individual from the community such as law enforcement officials, community agencies and program, shall normally be accommodated during the following time periods; 8:15am to 10:15 am, 12:45pm to 2:15pm and 6:30 pm to 10:30pm. Attorneys do not need to pre-schedule. All other professional visits need to be pre-scheduled through the Counselor Supervisors Office. The visiting rooms for professionals will be assigned first come, first serve.

"Thank God I can see Smalls..." I kept turning the pages until I got to page 28 and read the paragraph under Section H. – Telephone Regulations:

1. Telephone calls are only permitted between 9:00 a.m. and 10:30 p.m. (9:00-10:30am; 12:00-2:30pm; 7:00-10:30pm)
2. Five (5) calls a day of 15 minute duration are authorized.
3. You are not permitted to make third party calls or calls to Department of Correction officials or to a victim of a crime you are charged.
4. Telephone calls are not permitted during facility lockdowns.

Once I read number 3, I started crying again. "Bazil..." I cried. I kept turning the pages until I got to page 29 and read the paragraph under Section 18. Court Trip:

A. You must wear your own clothing unless you have none, in which case you will wear the state-issue uniform.
B. By 4:00 a.m. of the day of court, you must have your personal property packed and your bed stripped. Take your property and your bedding, including towels, to the A&P Room. The facility is not responsible for any property you leave behind in your housing unit.
C. You are only permitted to take legal materials with you that pertain to the case at hand. These materials must be surrendered to the transporting staff during transit. The materials will be returned to you when you are in secure

lock-up at the court and, on the return, when you are back in the facility.

D. You will be subject to the use of restraints in accordance with Department policy. (Reference: A.D. 6.4, Transportation of Inmates).

E. A court lunch will be provided.

F. You are not permitted to obtain or receive any item from any person while on a court trip.

I groaned out loud when I got to page 30 and read Section 19. Orientation:

The next business day after admission to this facility, you will be required to attend an orientation session. The purpose of these sessions is to inform you of how the facility works, what your obligations are, and what programs and services are available. Counselors will answer any questions you may have. If you refuse to attend orientation a Disciplinary Report will be given to you by your unit officer. Under normal circumstances you can expect to be housed in a designated orientation unit for at least seven (7) days after being admitted to this facility.

I kept turning the pages until I got to page 33 and started reading Section 4. Speedy Trial:

Speedy trial is a petition from an inmate to the court having jurisdiction to initiate proceedings to dispose untried charges. There are three types of speedy trials that affect inmates in custody; (1) an inmate in custody solely because of charges pending in this state (C.G.S. Sec. 54-82m); (2) an inmate under sentence with untried charges pending in this state (C.G.S. Sec. 54-82c); (3) an inmate under sentence with untried charges pending in another state (C.G.S. Sec. 54- 186, Article III). To apply for a speedy trial under C.G.S. Sec. 54-82m, contact your attorney or initiate pro se. For the other speedy trial motions contact your counselor.

"Hmmmmm... maybe I can get a speedy trial..." I said as I smiled. I lay down on that hard ass bunk, closed my eyes, and dreamed of Bazil.

Chapter 9

When I woke up the following morning, I went through the motions, not really speaking to anyone. As soon as I heard the call for chow, I headed straight for the dining hall, silently praying for coffee. "Thank you Lord," I said. I was relieved when I saw the coffee. I didn't mind waiting in line. When it was my turn, I got my tray, went to sit down, and, as luck would have it, the next available seat was next to Burly...

"Damn!" I said out loud as I remembered the rules: You are required to sit in the seat next to the last occupied seat at each table. Skipping seats is not permitted...

"Sup Beautiee..." she said as she touched my hair...

"Stop touching me!" I screamed...

"Do we have a problem here?" the Deputy Warden asked as he came over...

"No problem here – ain't that right Beautiee?" she said as she put her arm around me...

"Yes there's a fuckin' problem – I keep telling her stop touching me but this Burly Bitch doesn't understand English!" I said as I got up...

"Sit back down!" the Deputy Warden yelled...

"May I please sit somewhere else? I don't want her touching me!"

"Sit back down as you were instructed – you only have 20 minutes – and you..." he said, turning to Burly... "Keep your hands to yourself – got it?"

"Yes sir," she answered as I ate. "Ooohhh... I like what them lips do..." she slurred as soon as the Deputy Warden was outta sight...

"So does my husband..." I said before I started drinking my coffee...

"I got a nice dildo I could fuck you with..."

"Ain't happening..."

"I bet your lips suck a mean pussy..."

"You'll never know..." I said as I got up to take my tray to the scullery...

"We'll see about that..."

"In your dreams..." I said as I continued walking away... until she caught up to me with a few friends...

"Yo Beautiee – what's your fuckin' problem?" she asked as she got in front of me and pushed me..."

"See – there you go touching me again – I said don't fuckin' touch me!"

"Beautiee – have you read the Inmate Handbook?" the Deputy Warden asked as he came over to us...

"Yes I have..."

"Did you specifically read the section on personal conduct?"

"Yes I did..."

"Do you understand you are violating the personal code of conduct by using profanity?"

"I understand..." I sighed...

"Very well – come with me..." he said as he took me by the arm and out into the corridor... "Beautiee – listen to me..."

"Okay..."

"I need you to follow the rules to the letter – they know who you are – and they're just looking for an excuse to keep you in here..."

"Well – if that's the case – I already gave them one..."

"What happened?"

"That Burly Bitch came into my cell last night – I told her not to touch me – she tried to kiss me – and I stomped her ass!"

"Were there witnesses?"

"Yes – plenty!"

"Okay – we'll get her on violating the code of conduct for making sexually suggestive remarks and gestures towards you – but you have to stop using profanity – they'll use any little thing against you in here..."

"Shit!"

"Beautiee! What the fuck did I just say?"

"I'on know – what the fuck did you just say?" I laughed...

"I'll see you later..." he laughed as he went to get Burly...

"I got somethin' for you Beautiee..." I heard her say as he took her by the arm and down the corridor.

"Oh shit – Orientation!" I said out loud as I ran to keep from getting disciplinary action...

Smalls came to see me after orientation and I couldn't wait to be alone with him so we could talk. "How'd your first night go?" he asked.

"It was one of the worst nights of my life!"

"I'm sorry Beautiee. How'd you sleep?"

"I slept without my husband!" I snapped. "I need conjugal visits..."

"You've only been in here for one night..." Smalls laughed - but I was dead serious...

"I said I need conjugal visits!" I screamed in his face as I grabbed his jacket with both hands...

"Beautiee..." Smalls gritted between his teeth... "If you don't take your hands off me I'm about to forget who I'm talking too...

"I'm sorry..." I cried as I collapsed into his arms...

"It's okay... but I need you to hold it together... I gotchu... but you can't come at me like that..."

"I know... but I'm in trouble..."

"What happened?" Smalls asked as he sat down beside me...

"Can you get me conjugal visits? Please?" I asked, completely ignoring his question...

"If it were that easy Bazil would be here with you now..."

"So you can't?"

"This ain't like it is on TV Beautiee..." Smalls sighed...

"What do you mean?"

"Conjugal visits are only allowed in 4 states: California, Connecticut, New York, and Washington..."

"Thank God I'm in Connecticut..." I breathed...

"Conjugal visits were originally set up to preserve families... and you and Bazil don't have any children..."

"Oh my God..."

"You have to go on a waiting list..."

"What the hell?"

"You have to have impeccable prison behavior..."

"Oh damn... I'm fucked..."

"And... you have to be incarcerated for at least 90 days..."

"What the hell am I gonna do?"

"Beautiee – it's only 3 months..."

"I haven't slept alone since we've been married... I need my husband..." I whispered as I started crying again...

"Once you're approved, you can get visits from 24 hours to 3 days, once a month..."

"I hope I'm not in here too long..."

"Beautiee – I need you to listen to me..."

"Okay..."

"You'll be strip-searched and piss tested going in... and coming out..."

"Oh my God..."

"Once you close the door behind you, you get interrupted..."

"Interrupted?"

"They call you to come out when they do their rounds... just like when you're in your cell..."

"What?"

"And you have to come out so they can see you..."

"Damn..."

"There's also a tower above you – and the tower officer verifies you've been accounted for – and if you're on medication, they bring it to you..."

"Never mind... I'll just deal with it... at least Bazil can visit me every day... right?" Smalls didn't answer me. He just sighed and shook his head no...

"I can't even get visitation?" Now I was mad – and Smalls was about to get it... "This some straight bullshit!" I yelled. Smalls turned around with a 'who the fuck do you think you talkin' to' look on his face – but I didn't give a fuck... "If I were a registered sex offender or a child molester I could see friends, family, and have supervised visits with children..." Smalls tried to get me to quiet down by pointing to the door but I didn't give a fuck... "but they have a bug up their ass when it comes to me and Bazil so instead of going to the bathroom, taking a shit, and flushing the toilet like everyone else – they're denying me visitation – I still have rights dammit!" I screamed. Smalls looked at me with his eyes turned to slits. He stood up, closed his briefcase, and proceeded to walk past me... "Where the fuck do you think you're going?" I asked...

"I don't have to put up with this shit!" he yelled.

"Are you fuckin' kidding me right now? I'm stuck in here – my bail was revoked – I can't get any visitation – and you're mad because I'm upset?"

"I told you about comin' at me like that..."

"You're the only person I'm allowed to talk to!"

"I didn't do this shit to you!"

"I never said you did – but you're my attorney – and my rights are being violated – and I can't defend myself..." I said with tears in my eyes...

"You're right... I'm sorry..." Smalls said as he sat back down... "I'm just not in a good place right now..."

"What's wrong?"

"It has nothing to do with you..."

"I know..."

"Let's get back to your situation..."

"Let's not..."

"Beautiee... I can't sit here all day..."

"The hell you can't," I laughed "You're the only one I have permission to talk to... and I have questions... and you get paid by the hour... so let's talk..."

"Well... you can't see Bazil because..."

"Smalls?" I interrupted...

"Yes Beautiee?"

"What's wrong?" I asked as I took his hand. Smalls didn't answer me right away. His eyes started tearing up and I wrapped my arm around him...

"She wants a divorce..." I didn't say anything. I just kept my arm around him and held his hand... "I wish she was more like you..." he whispered...

"Me?" I asked in surprise...

"You love Bazil with everything in you – you're willing to fight for him... and you'll drag a Bitch with the quickness if a Bitch try and take him..." he laughed...

"Damn right I will..." I laughed...

"Don't tell Bazil..."

"Why not?"

"I don't want him to know..."

"That's your brother..."

"I know..."

"He'll be there for you..."

"I know... that's what I'm afraid of..."

"Why would you be afraid to let Bazil be there for you?"

"Because... he told her if she ever hurt me... he'd kill her..." I didn't respond. I just continued to hold his hand for a few moments... and then I changed the subject...

"So why can't I see Bazil?"

"When you're incarcerated, visitor's need to fill out an application. Once the application is approved, they're put on the list of approved visitors."

"That's bullshit – I didn't need to fill out an application to go see my cousin when he got locked up!"

"You're in here for 3 capital offenses Beautiee."

"I know..."

"So Bazil's application was denied for two reasons..."

"Okay..."

"He had a prior conviction... and... because he served time in this facility..." Smalls hesitated...

"What is it Smalls?"

"He's considered a security risk..." Smalls sighed.

"Can they do this?"

"Yes Beautiee... they can..."

"When's my next court date?"

"They're in the process of selecting jurors now..."

"How long will it take?"

"Connecticut isn't like other states..."

"I don't understand..."

"Connecticut has something called 'Individual Voir Dire' – this means the lawyers on both sides are allowed to question jurors individually and outside the presence of other jurors. It helps us exclude people we think are bias or can't be impartial."

"That can be to my benefit right?"

"If you were married to anybody but Bazil..." Smalls sighed.

"Oh my God..." I whispered.

"Have a little faith Beautiee..." Smalls said as he took my hand...

"How much longer?" I asked with tears in my eyes...

"We should be done in about a week..."

"So then I'll go to trial soon?"

"It could be a couple of weeks... or a couple of months..."

"Oh my God..."

"I'll do everything I can Beautiee..."

"How's Bazil?"

"Honestly... I'd rather be here with you..."

"That bad huh?"

"That bad..."

"You almost done in there?" The officer yelled...

"Why?" Smalls asked...

"You been in there a long time..."

"So what?"

"So she isn't entitled to preferential treatment – she needs to be back in her cell..."

"You got somewhere you need to be?"

"As a matter-of-fact... I do..."

"Sucks to be you then – I'll be done when I'm done!" Smalls yelled. I put my hand over my mouth to keep from laughing out loud. "Do you have any more questions?" Smalls asked...

"No..."

"Is there anything else I can do for you?"

"Yes..." I answered as I stood up and pulled him into a hug...

"I love you too Beautiee..."

"Smalls?"

"Yes Beautiee?"

"If she can't see what a good man you are... she doesn't deserve you..." I said as I kissed him on the cheek...

"Thank you Beautiee – Yo guard – I'm done..."

"'Bout fuckin' time!" he growled as he opened the door...

"Beautiee – I'll see you soon – have a good evening officer – what's your name?"

"Thompson..."

"What's your first name?"

"Good night Mr. Smalls," he answered ignoring Smalls question as he closed the door behind him and came towards me...

"Ummmmm... shouldn't I be going back to my cell?" I asked nervously...

"What's your hurry?" he asked as he walked me backwards into the corner..."

"Well... I thought you had somewhere to be... I wouldn't want to hold you up..."

"Mmmmm... you're beautiful... most women come in here and look like shit without make-up... but you... you're a natural beauty..." he said as he came closer. I couldn't move. He leaned in to kiss me and I tried to be gentle as I pushed him away from me...

"Thank you... I appreciate the compliment... maybe I should go back to my cell now..."

"In a bit... I'd like to get better acquainted..." he whispered as he pulled me into a kiss...

"I'm not interested in getting better acquainted!" I snapped as I pushed him away from me...

"Let me make myself clear..." he said as he pushed me back onto the corner... "I didn't ask you if you were interested in getting better acquainted – I said I'd like to get better acquainted!" He pulled me into a kiss again, sliding his hands up and down my back and down to my ass...

"My husband is going to have a problem with us getting acquainted..." I said as I pushed him away from me again...

"Fuck your husband – as long as you're in here – I'm your husband! Do I make myself clear?" he asked as he came towards me again...

"Perfectly..." I whispered...

"Good... now bring your ass here..." he said as he pulled me into a hug and started kissing me on my neck... "So... just to be clear... who's your husband?" he asked as he began massaging my breast...

"Bazil Osgood..." I answered with tears in my eyes...

"Oh my God... I'm... I'm sorry... he gasped as he backed away from me... "Let's get you back to your cell – come with me..." he stammered as he flew out the room. I ran down the corridor to catch up to him... "What's your hurry?" I thought you wanted to get better acquainted?"

"I got somewhere I gotta be!" he stammered as he hurried to unlock the cell..."

"Good night Officer Thompson..."

"Good night Mrs. Osgood!" he said as he locked the cell and hurried down the corridor.

Chapter 10

"Good afternoon, Bridgeport Correctional Center, how may I help you?"

"Hello Amonda," Bazil answered...

"Who's this?"

"Amonda Hannah... this is Bazil Osgood..."

"Hello Mr. Osgood... let me get Deputy Warden Nathan Hein... one moment..."

"Amonda?"

"Yes Mr. Osgood?"

"I'd rather speak to the Warden if you don't mind..."

"Actually I do... I'll get Deputy Warden Hein for you – one moment please..." she said as she transferred Bazil to Deputy Warden Hein...

"Mr. Osgood – how can I help you?" he asked as he answered the phone...

"I need to see my wife..."

"I'm sorry Mr. Osgood – we can't approve your visitation application due to..."

"Deputy Warden Hein right?" Bazil interrupted...

"Yes Mr. Osgood?"

"Have you suffered amnesia recently?"

"No Mr. Osgood..."

"Glad to hear it... how's your wife doing?"

"She's doing much better... thank you for asking..." he answered nervously...

"That's wonderful..." Bazil said...

"How are you Mr. Osgood?"

"I'm lucky to be alive... as I'm sure you know..."

"And how is your wife?"

"Well... since you asked... she's not doing too well..."

"I'm sorry to hear that – if there's anything we can do for her..."

"You know damn well what you can do for her!" Bazil interrupted...

"I'm getting another call Mr. Osgood – I have to go now – nice chatting with you..." he said nervously as he rushed off the phone...

"I'll see you soon Beautiee..." Bazil said out loud to himself as he smiled...

"Deputy Warden Hein – how may I help you?"

"Hey Nathan – it's Smalls..."

"Yes Smalls?"

"You don't sound like you're happy to hear from me...

"Look Smalls – I already know why you're calling – I'ma tell you the same thing I told Mr. Osgood – there's nothing I can do about his visitation application!" Smalls bust out laughing, which annoyed the hell out of Deputy Warden Hein...

"Who the fuck are you laughing at?"

"Wait... I can't... Oh God... Haaa.....
Haaa..... Haaa...."

"You think this shit's funny?"

"Nathan... stop... I can't..."

"I'm so fuckin' sick of you, Bazil Osgood,
and his wife – he may run you but that mutha
fucka don't run shit over here!"

"Yes he does..." Smalls laughed..."and
that's why you're mad..."

"That's it – fuck this!" Deputy Warden
Hein said as he slammed the phone down... and
then it rang again..."

"Deputy Warden Hein – how may I help
you?"

"You ready to talk now?" Smalls laughed.

"Jesus... yes Smalls – what can I do for
you?"

"See? That wasn't so hard was it?"

"Smalls you're really testing my
patience..."

"Nathan – it's not that serious..." he
laughed...

"What the fuck do you want?"

"Well..." Smalls laughed... "Since you
asked me so nicely... please let my client, Mrs.
Osgood, know I will see her in court tomorrow
morning at 9 a.m."

"What? Is that why you were calling?"

"Yes!" Smalls laughed...

"So you weren't calling to try and get us to
approve Mr. Osgood's visitation?"

"Nope."

"Damn – I'm sorry…"

"I know – it's cool…"

"I'll go give Mrs. Osgood the news – I'm sure she'll be happy to hear it…

"Thank you Nathan…"

"You're welcome – we'll talk soon…" Deputy Warden Hein said as he hung up the phone and got up to deal with the commotion he heard coming from the corridor….

"What's up now Bitch!" Burly yelled as she slammed the chair down on my head. Unbeknownst to Burly and everyone else, I'd had much practice in falling down while drunk only to get back up and laugh it off… and this dizziness I was feeling as I hit the floor was nothing compared to the rage that was boiling in my blood ever since she tried me…

"You tell me!" I screamed maniacally as I slid underneath the table, brought it up with my body, slammed it down on her, and stood on top of it, using the legs of the table as leverage so she couldn't get out from under it…

"Help… I can't breathe…" she choked as Deputy Warden Hein came running into the rec room…

"Get your ass down from there!" he yelled as he yanked me down off the table and threw me to the floor. I was enraged but I wasn't crazy enough to fight the Deputy Warden so I stayed right where he threw me and watched him lift the table up off Burly and console her…

"I'on know why she fuckin' wit' me!" she cried...

"Please – spare me the crocodile tears – you've been in the middle of shit since you got here..." he sighed as he shooed her away from him...

"That's fucked up! You must be fuckin' her!" she screamed...

"Thompson – take her to solitary!" Deputy Warden Hein yelled as he came towards me...

"You alright?" he asked as he extended his hand to help me up off the floor...

"I'll live..." I answered...

"You're bleeding – I'm taking you to the infirmary..." he said as he took me by the arm and escorted me out the rec room and down the corridor... "Listen to me..." he said as he turned me to face him and pushed me against the wall by my shoulders... "I'm trying to look out for you as best I can – but you can't afford to catch another charge – understand?"

"Yea..."

"I'll keep Burly in solitary for now but the max is 15 days – if you're still in here you have to avoid her at all costs..."

"How am I supposed to do that?"

"When you're in the rec room – make sure you're always facing the entrance – this way if she comes for you – you'll see her coming – she can't sneak you as long as you're facing her..."

"Okay..."

"I'm taking you to the infirmary – after you get checked out – you'll go back to your cell – unless you need to be taken to the hospital..."

"I hope not – my husband won't be happy about this..."

"Oh I already know..." he said as he escorted me into the infirmary...

"Nurse?"

"Yes Deupty?"

"Make sure she's okay – she needs to be in court tomorrow," he answered on his way out the door...

"Waaaiiitttt!" I yelled...

"Yes Beautiee?"

"I'm going to court tomorrow?"

"As long as you don't need to go the hospital – matter-of-fact – nurse, she's got an injury to her head – keep her here for tonight..."

"Yes sir..." the nurse acknowledged as she patted the bed for me to sit on so she could check my vitals...

"I'm going to court tomorrow..." I beamed as she took my blood pressure...

"Don't get your hopes up sweetie – you'll be back here tomorrow night..."

"Fuck you..." I thought to myself as she checked to see if I needed stiches. I couldn't contain my excitement.

"Make yourself comfortable – try to get some sleep..." she said as she propped a few pillows behind my head after pushing me back to lay down. I closed my eyes as if I were going to sleep and began fantasizing about Bazil...

Chapter 11

"Let's go Beautiee!" the nurse yelled as she turned on that bright neon light. I almost forgot where I was until I opened my eyes... "Deputy Hein will be here to escort you to breakfast – I'll see you later," she said as she went over to another prisoner...

"Well good morning to you too... Bitch..." I thought to myself as I jumped down off the bed and went towards the door...

"Good morning Beautiee – I hope you got some sleep – let's get you some breakfast..." Deputy Warden Hein said as he took me by the arm and escorted me down the corridor and past the rec room. I wasn't sure what was going on but I didn't ask questions – I just allowed him to lead me into another room with other prisoners... "Wait here – I'll be right back..." he said as he left the room...

"Hey... What's going on?" I asked a woman sitting next to me.

"We're all going to court," she answered.

"Oh... okay...," I smiled.

"I hope you like fried bacon, egg, and cheese on a roll 'cause that's all they had on the truck – and coffee light and sweet – this ain't a fuckin' restaurant so make due..." Deputy Warden Hein said as he placed a box of sandwiches and a box of coffees on the table...

"Oh my God – that smells so good!" I exclaimed as I took a sandwich and a cup of coffee...

"This is your first time huh?" she asked...

"Yea..." I answered as I started chewing...

"Hot damn! These virgins get younger and prettier," she laughed...

"Oh please – I'm nobody's virgin..." I laughed.

"I'm not talkin' about your virginity!" she laughed, "I'm talkin' about this being the first time you've been in jail! Haaaa..... Haaaaa....."

"Leave her alone Mary!" another woman said...

"It's okay..." I said... "I can't believe I thought you were talkin' about my virginity..." I laughed.

"What's your name pretty?" she asked.

"Beautiee."

"No shit! Your mother actually named you that?"

"Yea..."

"Well I'm Mary – it's nice to meet you..." she said as she extended her hand...

"Nice meeting you too..." I said as I shook her hand and started drinking coffee...

"Beautiee – let's go – now!" Deputy Warden Hein ordered as he walked back into the room. I stood up immediately, waiting for him to escort me to wherever I was going next. He took me by my arm and escorted me to another room, pushed me inside, came into the room, and closed the door behind him... "Sit down!" he ordered as he pointed to one of the chairs. He sat down in the other chair before he continued... "Stay away from Mary...

"Did I do something wrong?"

"Listen to me Beautiee – Mary's been in here for a long time – she gets cozy with newbies, gets them to trust her, then reports what she learns to the D.A. for perks and favors..."

"Okay..."

"Finish your coffee – you'll all be cuffed together when you leave here – you'll step up into the van – and you'll all sit together until we got to the court house – once we get to the court house you'll be escorted off the van and into the waiting room – once you get in the waiting room you'll be un-cuffed; however, when you're called you'll be re-cuffed with your hands in front of you and I'll escort you to the Bailiff. The Bailiff will sit you down at the table with your attorney and then your cuffs will come off.

"Will my husband be there?"

"I'm sure he'll be in the court room but he can't sit with you and your attorney."

"Okay..." I sighed...

"Listen to me Beautiee – and this is very important – I need you to behave yourself – no outbursts – no flailing arms and hands – and whatever you do – don't open your mouth unless instructed – you hear me?"

"Yea..."

"Okay – now let's go..." he said as he stood up, grabbed my arm, and escorted me back into the room with Mary and the others so we could get cuffed. When we got to the courthouse it was extremely chaotic – "This way! Hurry Up! Move!" They didn't give a damn that we were cuffed together – they just wanted us outta the way...

"Beautiee..." I heard... so I turned to look...

"Hey Keisha!" I beamed...

"We'll be inside..." she mouthed as she pointed to Courtroom A...

"Move it!" Deputy Warden Hein yelled as he pushed me into everyone else in front of me. When we got inside the waiting room he removed the cuffs before he spoke... "Sorry I was kinda rough – please don't take it personal – they're watching us all like a hawk – they have cameras and eyes everywhere – and Beautiee – don't ever speak to anyone you see coming or going – that's the worst thing you could possibly do to yourself – understand?"

"Yea..."

"Okay – Beautiee – you're up – stand up and extend your arms out in front of you..." He waited for me to do as instructed and then he cuffed my wrists before he continued... "I'm going to take you into the court room – the Bailiff will escort you to the table with your attorney — do you remember what we talked about?"

"Yea..."

"Okay then — let's go..." he said as he grabbed me by the arm and escorted me to the court room. Once inside, the Bailiff grabbed me by the arm and started to escort me to the table where Smalls was waiting for me with a smile, as well as the judge and the jury. I had all intentions of behaving myself but as soon as I saw Bazil my intentions went out the window along with my common sense...

"Bailiff! Get him!" the judge yelled as Bazil ran towards me and grabbed me up in his arms. Instinctively I lifted my arms over Bazil's head and wrapped my legs around his waist which cause us to fall to the floor... "Bailiff! What the hell's a matter with you! I said get him!" Bazil and I were kissing profusely. He was the oxygen I needed and in that moment I didn't give a damn about the judge, the Bailiff, or the jury — I was breathing — for the first time in days I could breathe without being afraid it would be my last breath — for the first time in days I could breathe in... breathe out... and breath in again. Bazil held me against him as we continued kissing and my cuffed wrists were underneath him so there was no way the Bailiff could follow the judge's order. Two officers came running down towards the bench as the Bailiff turned us on our side so he could un-cuff me and pull us apart...

"Please... don't hurt her!" Bazil cried as the court officers grabbed Bazil...

"You're the one that hurt your wife by pulling a stunt like that in my court room! Get 'em both outta here!" Judge Duffey boomed. Smalls stood up to plead my case but Bazil began pleading before he could...

"Your honor... please... I'm begging you..."

"You can fill out an application for visitation like everybody else..."

"My application was denied..." Bazil said as he started to cry. The court officers loosened their grip but didn't let him go...

"Is this true?" Judge Duffey asked Prosecutor Beverly...

"Yes it is..." Smalls answered...

"I'm not asking you Smalls..."

"Yes Your Honor..." Smalls acknowledged as he sat down...

"Yes – it's true Your Honor..." Beverly acknowledged. Judge Duffey sighed and shook his head before continuing...

"Mr. Osgood – when was the last time you saw your wife?"

"I haven't seen her since she was arrested..." Bazil answered while tears streamed down his face. No one said anything for a few moments. Judge Duffey shook his head, put his head in his hands, and then stood up before he spoke...

"Courts in recess – Smalls – Cogswell – in my chambers – Bailiff hold the defendant – Mr.

Osgood – go to the back and sit down – jurors please return to the waiting area until you're asked to return...

"Did you see that?" Juror #1 laughed.

"We all saw that – and we're not supposed to be discussing the case!" Juror #2 retorted...

"I'm talking about the way they were kissing – say what you want but that shit was hot!" Juror #1 said.

"I know – right?" Juror #3 laughed as Juror #1 and Juror #3 high-fived.

"I thought they looked ridiculous – rolling around on the floor like animals!" Juror #2 said.

"Oh Please – you wish your wife would jump your bones like that – hell – I wish my wife would jump my bones like that!" Juror #4 laughed...

"Me too!" Juror #5 agreed...

"What the hell is going on? Why was his application denied?" Judge Duffey asked Beverly...

"Well – Your Honor – it does say that applications may be denied due to prior convictions – and since he served time at the same facility – he's considered a security risk..."

"Beverly?"

"Yes Your Honor?"

"What exactly do you think the man's going to do - especially with his wife in custody?"

"That's not the point Your Honor..."

"Let me stop you before you wind up in contempt – that's exactly the point – and let me tell you something else – if you have a bug up your ass or a problem with Mr. Osgood – that's not my problem – however – if you cause a miss-trial because you can't be impartial and Mrs. Osgood files a complaint – that will be my problem – which will become your problem – am I clear?"

"Yes Your Honor..."

"Glad to hear it – now let's get started – I have a full calendar today and I'm already in a bad mood..." he said as he put his robe back on and they all headed back into the court room...

I watched as Judge Duffey came back into the court room along with the attorneys. Smalls walked past me and winked as he went to the table and sat down. After the prosecutor sat down the Bailiff spoke:

"All rise." Everyone stood up. "Department One of the Superior Court is now in session. Judge Duffey presiding. Please be seated."

Judge Duffey spoke... "Bailiff – please escort the jurors back into the court room. The Bailiff did as he was instructed. "Mr. Osgood – approach the bench." Bazil walked up to the bench and stood without speaking... "Mr. Osgood – you can remain in the court room as long as I don't hear a peep out of you – you are not to speak unless you are called to testify – other than that I don't want to hear a word from you – and I especially don't want another spectacle like I saw earlier – am I clear?"

"Yes Your Honor…" Bazil answered.

"Glad to hear it – now go sit in the back. The judge waited for Bazil to go sit down and then he spoke again… "Good morning, ladies and gentlemen. Calling the case of the People of the State of Connecticut versus Beautiee Osgood. Are both sides ready?"

"Ready for the People, Your Honor…" Beverly said.

"Ready for the Defense, Your Honor…" Smalls said.

"Will the clerk please swear in the jury?" Judge Duffey asked…

"Will the jury please stand and raise your right hand?" The clerk asked. After the jurors were standing she continued… "Do each of you swear that you will fairly try the case before this court, and that you will return a true verdict according to the evidence and the instructions of the court, so help you, God? Please say "I do". The jurors said "I do" unison. "You may be seated."

Chapter 12

Beverly's Opening Statement

"Your Honor and ladies and gentlemen of the jury,

The defendant has been charged with the attempted murder of her husband, Bazil Osgood, the murder of Sonia Santos, and the murder of Trevor Joseph. The evidence will show that on January 13, 2019, the defendant invited her lover, Sonia Santos over to her home as well as her husband's lover, Trevor Joseph to set them all up to be killed. The evidence will also show that her husband, Bazil Osgood, her lover, Sonia Santos, and her husband's lover, Trevor Joseph, were all shot with the same gun. The defendant's fingerprints were on the gun used to shoot her husband, Bazil Osgood, her lover, Sonia Santos, and her husband's lover, Trevor Joseph. The evidence I present will prove to you that the defendant is guilty as charged."

Smalls's Opening Statement

"Your Honor and ladies and gentlemen of the jury,

Under the law my client is presumed innocent until proven guilty. During this trial, you will hear no real evidence against my client. You will come to know the truth: that my client, Beautiee Osgood, loves her husband. You will also find out that my client invited her lover, Sonia Santos, over to have a threesome with her husband – she did not invite her lover over to kill her, nor did she intend to kill her husband. You will also find out that her husband's lover, Trevor Joseph, was never invited. You will also come to know that my client shot her husband's lover, Trevor Joseph, because she feared for her life – especially after he shot her husband – therefore; my client is not guilty."

"Beverly – you may call your first witness..." Judge Duffey said.

"Thank you Your Honor – I call Joselyn Logan."

"Oh shit!" I heard someone say from the back of the court room. I looked straight ahead but I could feel Bazil watching me and I knew he was worried about what Joselyn was going to say...

"Please state your name for the record..." Judge Duffey instructed...

"Joselyn Logan."

"Please raise your right hand and place your left hand on the bible..." Judge Duffey instructed as the court clerk held the Bible... "Do you swear, under penalty of perjury, that the testimony you are about to give shall be the truth, the whole truth, and nothing but the truth?"

"I swear, under penalty of perjury, that the testimony I am about to give shall be the truth, the whole truth, and nothing but the truth."

"Thank you Joselyn – but in the future – you can simply answer I do..."

"Oh – Okay – I thought I was already married!" Joselyn laughed along with the jurors and everyone else in the court room... except Beverly...

"That was funny Joselyn – however – this is not – understand?" Beverly retorted...

"Objection – that's a witness – not her child..." Small said.

"I know that's right!" Keisha yelled out before quickly putting her hand ovr her mouth...

"Sustained – easy Beverly..." Judge Duffey ordered...

"Mrs. Logan where you at work on December 17, 2018?"

"Yes I was."

"Did you witness an altercation between the defendant and MaryJane LaRue?"

"Yes... I did..."

"Please tell the court what you witnessed..."

"Well... I'm sorry Mrs. Osgood..."

"Your Honor – please instruct the witness to address the court and not the defendant..." Beverly said.

"Mrs. Logan – please address the court and not the defendant..." Judge Duffey ordered...

"Okay..." Joselyn answered as tears streamed down her cheeks. Sam ran up to the witness box to give his wife a tissue and console her...

"Are you okay to continue?" Judge Duffey asked as Sam went to sit back down...

"Yes Your Honor..." Joselyn answered...

"Very well – please answer the question..." Judge Duffey ordered. Joselyn sighed before continuing...

"Mrs. Osgood dragged MaryJane down the hall by her hair... and threw her out the door..." Most of the jury gasped – some of them laughed...

"Did the defendant say anything to MaryJane LaRue after she was thrown out?" Beverly asked. Joselyn started crying again before answering...

"Mrs. Osgood told her if she caught her on the premises again... she would kill her..."

The jury gasped again...

"Mrs. Logan – to clarify – is it your testimony that the defendant threatened MaryJane LaRue and told her she would kill her if she were caught back on the premises?"

"Yes..." Joselyn acknowledged.

"Thank you Mrs. Logan – nothing further..." Beverly said as she looked over at Smalls and then said, "Your Witness..." before sitting down.

"How are you Mrs. Logan?" Smalls asked as he stood up...

"I'm okay..."

"Can I get you some water?"

"No thank you..."

"Okay – Mrs. Logan – prior to the altercation you witnessed with the defendant – did you have a conversation with MaryJane LaRue?"

"Yes I did..."

"Where did this conversation take place?"

"In the ladies room."

"Did you discuss the defendant?"

"Yes we did."

"What – if anything – did MaryJane LaRue say to you in the ladies room?"

"She called Mrs. Osgood a Bitch and she said she was going to have to check Mrs. Osgood and put her in her place like she did Mr. Osgood's first wife." The jury gasped... Smalls smiled along with Joselyn's husband Sam and Bazil as Beverly put her head in her hands before Smalls continued...

"Did anyone hear your conversation in the ladies room?"

"Yes."

"Who heard your conversation?"

"My mother and Mrs. Osgood."

"Mrs. Logan – to be clear – is it your testimony that your mother and the defendant heard your conversation in the ladies room?"

"Yes."

"Hmmmmm... I would'a threw her ass out too..." Smalls mumbled...

"Objection – move to strike!" Beverly yelled...

"Objection sustained – the jury will disregard that last comment – Smalls don't ever do that in my court..."

"Yes Your Honor – I apologize..." Smalls smirked as he looked at Beverly and sat down.

"Re-direct?" Judge Duffey asked.

"No Your Honor..." Beverly answered...

"The witness may be excused..." Judge Duffey said. Joselyn got up from the witness box and joined her husband behind Smalls.

"I'm proud of you..." Sam whispered as he took her hand...

"Really? I didn't want to say all that..." Joselyn whispered. Bazil put his hand on Joselyn's shoulder and smiled...

"Mr. Osgood – please move to the back of the court as you were instructed earlier – don't let me have to remind you again!" Judge Duffey growled...

"Yes Your Honor – sorry..." Bazil said as he got up and went to the back of the court room with Troy & Keisha. Judge Duffy watched as

Keisha took Bazil's hand for a few moments before he spoke...

"Court will be in recess for 30 minutes – Bailiff – please escort the jurors to the waiting room – everyone else may remain seated in the court room or you can go out for coffee..." Judge Duffey said as he got up and left the bench to go to his chambers...

"You okay?" Smalls whispered to me so Beverly couldn't hear our conversation...

"I'm fine..." I sighed.

"I know you're happy 'cause you got to see Bazil but you need to stay focused – don't smile – don't do anything – just sit here... with me..." he whispered as he pulled me into a hug and slipped me a pad and pen as if he was reading my mind...

"Hey My Thirst Quencher..." I wrote...

"I'm sorry to tell you this – but after my arrest, Smalls came to see me. When he left – Officer Thompson came in the room to see me. I asked to go back to my cell but Officer Thompson said he wanted to get better acquainted. I told him my husband wouldn't like it but he said fuck your husband – while you're in here – I'm your husband! I pushed him away from me but he grabbed me, he kissed me, and told me he wasn't asking my permission... and then he groped my breast! As he was feeling my breast he asked me if he made himself clear and I told him he made himself perfectly clear. He asked me again who my husband was but instead of saying his name I said your name – he got scared, apologized, and hurried me back to my cell. I didn't report it and I don't want to report it – I'm already going through enough dealing with the Burly Bitch who tried to push up on me talkin' 'bout she was going to fuck me with a dildo but instead she chose to hit me upside my head with a chair because I embarrassed her ass – don't worry too much about that – I brought a table down on top of her and Deputy Warden Hein put her in solitary so she won't fuck with me again for the moment – I love you so much – I'm trying to be strong but I don't know how much more I can take." When I finished writing, I slid the pad and pen back to Smalls...

"Something's wrong..." Bazil whispered...
"Why you say that?" Troy asked...
"Look at Smalls – he's pissed – something's wrong – I can feel it...

"You need to report this mutha fucka!" Smalls wrote before passing the pad back to me... I snatched the pen and responded... "No!" and then slammed the pen down on the pad...

"See – I told you – something's wrong – my wife's in trouble..." Bazil whispered as he started to cry...
"Le'me go find out what's up..." Keisha said as she walked up towards Smalls...

"Miss – please return to your seat until you're called as a witness..." the Bailiff ordered...

"Shit!" Keisha said as she went to sit back down. Bazil watched intently as Smalls tore the paper off the pad, folded it, and put it in his left pocket. Smalls then took a pencil out of his briefcase, went across the paper with the pencil to highlight all the imprints on the page, tore that paper off the pad, and put it in his right pocket...

"I'll be right back – I'm going to the bathroom..." Smalls said deliberately...

"I need to go too – I haven't used the bathroom since I drank coffee..." I said just as deliberately...

"You can't go right now..." the Bailiff said...

"Please – I won't run – I just need to pee – you have cameras everywhere..."

"Very well – I'll escort you to the bathroom..." he said as he walked over to the table and un-cuffed me...

"Really?" Smalls said, agitated... "I'll escort my client to the bathroom!"

"Sir – I can't let you do that..." the Bailiff said...

"He's right..." Beverly added...

"Yo – check it – I'm taking my client to the fuckin' bathroom – to pee! Let's go Beautiee!" Smalls said as he snatched me by the arm, pulled me up out the chair, and marched me down towards the back of the court room, past Bazil,

Keisha, Troy, Sam, and Joselyn – and out the door into the corridor...

"Hey – wait a minute – you can't do that!" another Bailiff yelled...

"What? What the fuck am I doing? I'm her attorney! Do you really think I would jeopardize my client's freedom?" Smalls yelled...

"I'm sorry sir – she needs to be escorted inside the bathroom and out..." the Bailiff said...

"And I'll do that – now can we go or should she just pee right here?"

"Fine – but make sure she doesn't try anything..."

"Whatever – c'mon Beautiee – hurry up 'cause I gotta pee too..." Smalls said as he deliberately pushed me into the men's room... "Listen – go down to the last stall and close the door – hopefully Bazil will get the hint and come look for you – give him this..." he said as he handed me the paper form his right pocket... "I'm going to wait by the door to make sure you don't try anything – but I gotta pee first – and if you really gotta pee – leave it in the toilet in case they wanna check..." he laughed as he went into another stall...

"Shit – Smalls you in here?" Bazil asked as he came into the men's room...

"Yea Bazil – I'll be out in a minute..." Smalls answered... and then Bazil saw me as I came out the stall...

"Beautiee..." Bazil said as he came towards me..."

"Hey my Thirst Quencher..." I sighed as we fully embraced. Bazil began kissing me forcefully and I had no objection. I opened my mouth further and welcomed his tongue. Bazil moved his right arm up, pulled me closer with his left, and bent me back on the sink as we continued kissing feverishly...

"Beautiee – let's go – they'll come looking for us..." Smalls said as he started tugging at my arm...

"I love you so much it hurts..." Bazil said as he continued to hold me...

"I love you too..." I said as I put the folded paper Smalls gave me into Bazil's pocket...

"Beautiee – we gotta go..." Smalls said, tugging at my arm...

"We're gonna get through this Beautiee..." Bazil said as he kissed me again..."

"You promise?" I asked as I kissed him back...

"I promise..." Bazil answered as he kissed me again...

"And you never make a promise you can't keep... right?" I asked through tear-soaked eyes...

"Right..." Bazil answered as he kissed my eyes and my tears...

"Beautiee..." Smalls said as he tugged my arm again...

"I'm coming..." I sighed as I let go of Bazil and allowed Smalls to escort me back to the court room...

"All rise..."the Bailiff said. Everyone stood up. "Department One of the Superior Court is now in session. Judge Duffey presiding. Please be seated."

"Calling the case of the People of the State of Connecticut versus Beautiee Osgood. Are both sides ready?"

"Ready for the People, Your Honor..." Beverly said.

"Ready for the Defense, Your Honor..." Smalls said.

"Welcome back Mrs. Osgood," Judge Duffey said sarcastically...

"I'm sorry Your Honor – I had to pee..." The jurors laughed along with Keisha, Troy, Sam, and Joselyn...

"Since your husband's not here, I'm guessing that's not all you had to do..." Judge Duffey said. I didn't say anything – I just sat down smiling... "I don't like to be kept waiting..." Judge Duffey said...

"It won't happen again Your Honor..." Smalls said...

"It better not..."

"Yes Your Honor."

"Beverly – are you ready to call your next witness?"

"Yes Your Honor – I call Sheila Henley." We all watched as Sheila went to the witness box.

"Please state your name for the record..." Judge Duffey instructed...

"Sheila Henley."

"Please raise your right hand and place your left hand on the bible..." Judge Duffey instructed as the court clerk held the bible... "Do you swear, under penalty of perjury, that the testimony you are about to give shall be the truth, the whole truth, and nothing but the truth?"

"I will..." Sheila said as she sat down.

"I guess you're already married?" Judge Duffey asked...

"I am..."

"Very well – Beverly – you may proceed..."

"Mrs. Henley – earlier today, Mrs. Logan testified that you over-heard a conversation between her and MaryJane LaRue – is that true?" Beverly asked...

"Yes it is..." Sheila answered...

"Would you please tell the court and the jury what you specifically heard?"

"I specifically heard MaryJane LaRue call Mrs. Osgood a Bitch and I specifically heard MaryJane LaRue tell my daughter that she was going to have to check Mrs. Osgood and put her in her place like she did Mr. Osgood's first wife."

"You didn't like MaryJane LaRue did you?"

"Objection..." Smalls said.

"Overruled – the witness may answer..." Judge Duffey ordered...

"No I didn't..."

"Could you please explain to the court why you didn't like MaryJane LaRue?"

"She was lazy, she passed most of her work to my daughter, and she walked around like she owned the place..."

"I see – what was Ms. LaRue's title?"

"The same as my daughter – Personal Assistant."

"Was Mr. Osgood having an affair with Ms. LaRue?"

"Objection!" Smalls yelled...

"Sustained..." Judge Duffey acknowledged...

"Withdrawn..." Beverly said... and then she continued... "Your daughter was promoted after Ms. LaRue was thrown out – wasn't she?"

"Yes she was..."

"Hmmmmm... how convenient..." Beverly said sarcastically...

"It had nothing to do with convenience – my daughter is loyal, dedicated, and works hard – she earned that promotion!"

"Isn't it true that your son-in-law – Samuel Logan – is also the Vice President of Osgood Publishing?"

"Yes – that's true..."

"So – to make sure I understood you correctly – your son-in-law is the Vice President at Osgood Publishing – your daughter – who also works there – gets promoted right after Ms. LaRue gets thrown out – and you never liked her – and you don't think any of this is a coincidence?"

"No – I don't think any of that is a coincidence…"

"Hmmmmm… interesting – your witness…" Beverly said to Smalls as she sat down…

"Mrs. Henley – you testified that you overheard the conversation in the bathroom between Ms. LaRue and your daughter – is that correct?"

"Yes it is…"

"Did you have any prior knowledge that Ms. LaRue felt animosity towards Mrs. Osgood?"

"Objection!" Beverly yelled.

"Overruled – the witness may answer…" Judge Duffey ordered…

"No I did not…"

"Did you know Ms. LaRue was in the bathroom?"

"No I did not…"

"Did Mrs. Osgood tell you that she was planning on promoting your daughter?"

"No she did not."

"Prior to Mrs. Osgood throwing Ms. LaRue out – did you have any discussion regarding Ms. LaRue with Mrs. Osgood, Mr. Osgood, or your son-in-law?"

"No I did not…"

"Thank you Mrs. Henley – I have no further questions…" Smalls said as he sat down…

"The witness is excused – I'm taking an early lunch – court is closed for lunch – please be back by 1 pm sharp!" Judge Duffey said as he put on his robe, stood up, and went into his chambers. I watched as the jurors exited the court room, then the clerk.

"Everyone needs to leave – court is closed..." the Bailiff ordered. Keisha, Troy, Joselyn, and Sam exited the court room. Bazil was nowhere in sight.

"I wish I could go to lunch too..." I sighed...

"Mrs. Osgood – you need to come with me..." the Bailiff said as he approached me...

"I need to speak with my attorney... please..."

"I'll escort you to the attorney-client room – your attorney can meet you there..." he said as he took me by the arm and pulled me up... "Sorry – I need to cuff you..." he said as he cuffed my hands.

"I'll see you in a few minutes – I'll treat you to lunch – be right back!" Smalls said as he ran out...

"This way Mrs. Osgood..." the Bailiff said as he led me down the corridor past the men's room, to the attorney-client room. "Wait here for your attorney – I'll see you back in the court room..." he said as he left...

"Beautiee..." Bazil whispered as he cracked the door...

"Bazil – don't come in..." I whispered...

"I'm not – I'm waiting for Smalls..."

"Okay..."

"I love you..."

"I love you too..."

"Bazil – you can't be here..." Smalls said...

"I know – I'm leaving – come by the house after court – we'll talk then..." Bazil said...

"Aaight bet – I'll see you tonight..." Smalls said as Bazil went down the hall and left the courthouse...

"Home at last..." Bazil said out loud after closing the door behind him... "Time to get something to eat, something to drink, and read Beautiee's love letter..." he sighed as he went into the kitchen, pulled out a loaf of Italian bread, turkey, ham, roast beef, pastrami, provolone cheese, American cheese, lettuce, tomato, Hellman's mayonnaise, mustard, and a can of Pepsi. "Damn I'm hungry..." he said out loud as he made a man's sandwich. When he was done, he opened the can of Pepsi, picked up the sandwich with one hand, took a huge bite, took the letter out of his pocket, sat down at the island, and started reading... "Oh Hell No!" he yelled as he pounded his fist into the table. He continued to eat and drink as he read that line again...

'I'm sorry to tell you this...'

'Officer Thompson wanted to get better acquainted...'

'Fuck your husband – While you're in here – I'm your husband!'

"Is that right Officer Thompson? We'll see about that!" Bazil gritted through his teeth as he continued reading...

'Grabbed me...'
'Kissed me...'
'Not asking permission...'
'Groped my breast...'
"Hmmmmm... it seems you have a propensity for touching what doesn't belong to you... I may have to teach you a lesson... and word has it – I'm a great teacher..." Bazil said out loud as he continued reading... "Oh – what's this? You actually apologized? You're sorry? Aaaa.... Haaa.... Haaa... Haaa.... Damn right you're sorry – I can't wait to hear it in person..." he gritted as he continued reading... "Beautiee..." he whispered as he started to cry...

'Hit me upside my head with a chair...'

"Beautiee..." Bazil said with a smile as he continued reading...

'Brought table down on top of her...'
'Deputy Warden Hein put her in solitary...'

"Thank you Deputy Hein..." Bazil said out loud as he finished his sandwich, finished his soda, and headed straight to the Milford Police Department.

"Okay Beautiee – I got some good ole fashioned comfort food – macaroni & cheese, fried chicken, collard greens, cornbread, and sweet tea..." he said as I tore the lid off and dove in... "I got me a plate too..." Smalls said as he started eating...

"Bazil didn't read my letter yet..."

"I know he didn't – he's too happy..."

"I'm scared..."

"I know – but I think we can beat this..."

"I'm not afraid of that... I'm afraid of Bazil..."

"I'm afraid too – I didn't even want to tell him but I had too – I'd wanna know if it was my wife..."

"He'd never forgive you if you didn't tell him..."

"That too..." he laughed... "But Beautiee – you need to file a complaint..."

"I can't..."

"Yes you can – I'll be with you every step of the way..."

"You can't be with me 24 hours..."

"I'll get you protective custody..."

"I'm already in hell – imagine what they'll do to me if I report it? I just wanna get through this so I can go home..." I said as I started to cry...

"I know Beautiee – I gotchu..." he said as he handed me a napkin – but once Bazil reads your letter they'll know..."

"So what?"

"So you can't afford to have your husband back in prison..."

"I know that too – what am I supposed to do?"

"Le'me ask you something – why didn't you tell me what was going on with Burly?" I bust out laughing... "What's so funny?"

"The way you say Burly..." I laughed...

"Is that her name?"

"That's my name for her – and when you see her – that'll be your name for her too – she makes Buckwheat from the Alphalfas look sexy!" I laughed...

"Damn – that's fucked up!" Smalls laughed – but I'm glad you fucked her up..."

"I had no choice – she would've kept coming for me..."

"Well – since Deputy Hein is lookin' out I won't push that issue – but Officer Thompson needs his ass beat!"

"Oh it's comin'!" I laughed...

"I know – that's what I'm afraid of..."

"Mr. Osgood – how are ya?" Sergeant Chandler asked as Bazil walked into the precinct...

"Lucky to be alive..." Bazil answered...

"What can I do for you?" Sergeant Chandler asked...

"Can we talk in private?" Bazil asked...

"Sure – come with me..." Sergeant Chandler said as Bazil followed him through the door and into another room... "Wait here – I'll be right back..." Sergeant Chandler said as he left Bazil alone in the room. Bazil surveyed the area while they were walking towards the room and spotted a flyer congratulating Officer Thompson on his promotion on the bulletin board. Unbeknownst to Sergeant Chandler, Bazil was on a mission... "Okay – what can I do for you?" Sergeant Chandler asked as he went to close the door...

"Please – leave it open – this won't take long..." Bazil said.

"Okay – does this have anything to do with Detective Jones testifying today?"

"Is Detective Jones is testifying today?"

"Yes she is – she left to be in court by 1 pm..."

"Oh – in that case – I'll be quick – I came here because I wanted to thank you for your professionalism and courtesy in dealing with my wife..."

"Are you feeling okay Mr. Osgood?" Sergeant Chandler said as he started feeling Bazil's forehead..."

"I'm feeling as well as can be expected..."

"Are you really here to thank me – or is there something else?"

"I'm just here to thank you – I have no ulterior motives – I would never do anything that would hurt my wife..."

"I believe that... Sergeant Chandler said as Officer Thompson came down the hall...

"Sergeant? You in here?" Officer Thompson yelled...

"Yea Thompson – What's up?"

"I'm heading back to Bridgeport – I'ma just head to the bathroom real quick – I'll see you later tonight when I get back..." This was music to Bazil's ears...

"Aaight – I'll see you later tonight..." Sergeant Chandler said...

"Sergeant – I need to get to court – can you show me where the bathroom is?" Bazil asked...

"Sure – down the hall, first right..."

"Thanks – I gotta go!" Bazil said as he jumped up from the table and made a beeline for the bathroom...

"Wooo hoo – damn I had to go!" Officer Thompson said as he flushed the toilet and came out the stall...

"Hello Officer Thompson..." Bazil said...

"I can explain..." Officer Thompson started to say..."

"Shhhhh..." Bazil whispered as he pushed Officer Thompson back into the sink and turned him around so Officer Thompson could see Bazil kissing him on the back of his neck in the mirror in front of him...

"Please Bazil... I'm sorry..."

"I'm sure you are..." Bazil breathed in his ear as he began to unbuckle Officer Thompson's belt...

"Oh God... Please Bazil... I swear... I didn't know... I'll never touch your wife again..." he pleaded...

"I know you won't..." Bazil said as he put his hand in Officer Thompson's pants, grabbed his dick and his balls... and squeezed... "Do you like this?" Bazil breathed in his ear...

"No... please don't do this..."

"What exactly is it that you don't want me to do?"

"Please... don't rape me..."

"Why not? Isn't that what you were planning on doing to my wife? Isn't that what you've been doing to all the female inmates?"

"I... I... I..."

"I have eyes... and ears... everywhere..." Bazil whispered in Officer Thompson's ear as he squeezed Officer Thompson's dick and balls tighter...

"Oh no... please..." Officer Thompson pleaded...

"Do you like having a dick... or would you prefer a catheter?" Bazil breathed in his ear...

"Please... I don't want a catheter..."

"If you ever touch my wife... or any other female inmate... and it gets back to me... and trust me... it will get back to me... and when it does... I'll find you... and I'll detach your dick and your balls from your body... do you understand?"

"Yes... it won't happen again... I swear..."

"Very well... I need to get to court now — you have a nice day... and say hello to Deputy

Warden Hein for me..." Bazil said as he let go of Officer Thompson's dick and balls, backed away from him, and turned him around to face him... and Officer Thompson pissed himself...

"Thompson! What are you still doing in here?" Sergeant Chandler yelled as he came into the bathroom...

"I... I... had an accident..." Officer Thompson stammered as Bazil turned on the water and washed his hands...

"Hein..." Deputy Hein answered...

"It's Bazil..."

"Bazil – how the hell did you get my private cell phone number?"

"That's not important..."

"What the hell do you want Bazil?"

"You have a problem named Officer Thompson – correct?"

"Oh God Bazil – what the hell did you do?"

"He touched my wife..."

"Oh God... Bazil... I'm sorry... please tell me he's still breathing..."

"He's still breathing..."

"Oh thank God – and thank you..."

"You're welcome – and thank you also..." Bazil said as he hung up and turned his cell phone off...

"It's 12:45 – let's get back before everyone else..." Smalls said as he got up to leave the room...

"Good idea – thanks for lunch..." I said as I got up and we left the room...

"All rise..."the Bailiff said. Everyone stood up. "Department One of the Superior Court is now in session. Judge Duffey presiding. Please be seated."

"Calling the case of the People of the State of Connecticut versus Beautiee Osgood. Are both sides ready?"

"Ready for the People, Your Honor..." Beverly said.

"Ready for the Defense, Your Honor..." Smalls said.

"Thank you all for being prompt..." Judge Duffey said as he sat down... Beverly – you may call your next witness..."

"Thank you Your Honor – I call Detective Katina Jones."

Chapter 13

"Please state your name for the record..." Judge Duffey instructed...

"Katina Jones."

"Please raise your right hand and place your left hand on the bible..." Judge Duffey instructed as the court clerk held the Bible... "Do you swear, under penalty of perjury, that the testimony you are about to give shall be the truth, the whole truth, and nothing but the truth?"

"I do..." Detective Jones said as she sat down.

"Very well – Beverly – you may proceed..."

"Detective Jones – did you receive a call for possible domestic violence at the defendant's address on December 23, 2018 at around 9 p.m.?"

"Yes I did."

"When you arrived, what – if anything did you witness?"

"I received a call for possible domestic violence at the defendant's home. When I arrived, I knocked on the door, asked if I could come in, and I was allowed inside."

"What – if anything – did you observe?"

"The defendant appeared to be upset."

"Did you determine that any domestic violence had occurred?"

"Yes – I did."

"How did you determine that domestic violence had occurred?"

"I asked the defendant if everything was okay and she told me that she and her husband had a fight…" I listened intently as the jurors started whispering…

"Your initial report also indicated that someone heard gun shots – is that true?"

"Yes it is."

"Did you ask the defendant about gun shots specifically?"

"Yes I did."

"What was her response?"

"She told me they were watching Law & Order…" The jurors laughed – but Judge Duffey wasn't amused…

"Did the defendant appear to be hurt?"

"No – she didn't."

"What did you do after you were done with your conversation?"

"I gave her my card, and then I left."

"Thank you Detective – your witness…" Beverly said before she sat down…

"Detective Jones – how are you?" Smalls asked…

"I'm fine…"

"Glad to hear it – on the night in question – did you recover a gun from the defendant's home?"

"No I didn't..." she sighed...

"Was Mr. Osgood home at the time?"

"Yes he was."

"Did he tell you his wife tried to kill him?"

"No he did not."

"Did he want to press charges?"

"No he did not."

"One more question – isn't it true that you told the defendant to be careful because her husband is dangerous?" I smiled as Beverly put her head in her hands and I heard the jurors gasp...

"Yes... that's true – I did tell the defendant that..."

"So – to be clear – it's your testimony that the defendant didn't appear to be hurt – her husband didn't want to press charges – but yet – you warned the defendant to be careful because her husband is dangerous?"

"Yes."

"So – he's dangerous but she's on trial for murder..."

"Objection!" Beverly yelled.

"Sustained..." Judge Duffey said.

"Withdrawn – I'm done!" Smalls said sarcastically as he threw up his hands and sat down...

"The witness is excused – Beverly – you may call your next witness..." Judge Duffey said.

"Thank you Your Honor – I call Beautiee Osgood..." The jury gasped.

"Are you sure you want to do this?" Smalls asked me before I went up to the witness box...

"Yes..." I answered. I was scared but the jury only saw sadness. I could hear the jurors whispering as I went up to the witness box...

"Please state your name for the record..." Judge Duffey instructed...

"Mrs. Beautiee Osgood."

"Please raise your right hand and place your left hand on the bible..." Judge Duffey instructed as the court clerk held the Bible... "Do you swear, under penalty of perjury, that the testimony you are about to give shall be the truth, the whole truth, and nothing but the truth?"

"Yes... I swear..." I said as I sat down.

"Very well – Beverly – you may proceed..."

"How are you Beautiee?" Beverly asked...

"Please call me Mrs. Osgood..."

"Very well – on the first night Detective Jones came to your home – what event transpired?"

"My husband and I were fighting and my neighbor called the police..."

"How you know it was me?" Keisha yelled out. Smalls laughed along with the jury.

"What were you fighting about?"

"Bazil..." I whispered as I began to tear up...

"Mr. Osgood – please go back to your seat!" Judge Duffey ordered.

"I'm just giving my wife some tissues your honor..." Bazil said as he placed the tissues on the table in front of Smalls before returning to the back of the court room with Troy and Keisha.

"We're heading back to the office – call us if you need us..." Sam whispered to Bazil as he got up to leave along with Joselyn and Sheila...

"Your honor – please order the witness to answer the question!" Beverly snapped...

"Please answer the question..." Judge Duffey ordered...

"He... he... cheated on me..." I cried. The jurors gasped. Smalls got up to bring me tissues, and then he sat back at the table...

"Your husband?" Beverly asked...

"Yes..." I answered as I wiped my eyes. I looked toward the back of the court room at Bazil. He was crying and I felt terrible...

"How did you know your husband was cheating on you?"

"I caught them..." I cried.

"Who did you catch your husband cheating on you with?"

"Bazil... I'm sorry..." I cried...

"Your honor..." Beverly started to say...

"Mrs. Osgood – please do not address your husband while giving testimony..." Judge Duffey ordered...

"My husband was cheating on me with Trevor..." I cried. The jurors gasped. I looked towards the back at Bazil. I hated myself but this was necessary – at least I thought so – I prayed so...

"So is it your testimony that you had a fight with your husband because you caught him cheating on you with Trevor?"

"No..."

"Mrs. Osgood – I don't understand..."

"We were fighting because... Bazil was angry with me..."

"Why was your husband angry with you?"

"Because... after I caught Bazil sleeping with Trevor..." I had to stop and gather myself. I kept looking back at Bazil praying he'd forgive me...

"Go on Mrs. Osgood..."

"I slept with Trevor too..." The jurors gasped. I kept looking back at Bazil. He was still crying. I wanted to run to him and beg for forgiveness...

"Wow – I didn't expect that..." Beverly said...

"Is that a question?" Smalls asked.

"Withdrawn – Mrs. Osgood – are you telling us you had a physical altercation with your husband because you slept with his lover?"

"That's part of it..." I answered...

"Please tell the court the other part..." Beverly laughed...

"Objection!" Smalls yelled...

"What's your objection Smalls?" Judge Duffey asked...

"This isn't funny – why is she laughing?"

"Sustained – Mrs. Osgood – please continue..."

"I wanted some wine and I went into the kitchen – but Bazil poured my wine out so I wanted to leave... and Bazil wouldn't let me..."

"What happened next?" Beverly asked...

"Bazil grabbed me... he threw me into the counter... and hurt my back..."

"I'm sorry Beautiee..." Bazil said from the back of the court room...

"Mr. Osgood – please be quiet!" Judge Duffey ordered...

"What – if anything – happened next?" Beverly asked...

"I grabbed a knife out of the holder..." I answered as I started crying again..." and I stabbed him!" I said as I broke down crying. Bazil was crying right along with me.

"I have no further question..." Beverly said with a smile as she sat down... "Your witness..." she said as Smalls got up...

"Here Beautiee..." Smalls said as he handed me some tissues. He waited for me to blow my nose, wipe my tears, and compose myself before he continued... "That was pretty intense – wasn't it?"

"Yes..."

"You testified you stabbed your husband – is that right?"

"Yes... it is..." I answered as I started crying again...

"Where did you stab your husband?"

"I stabbed him... in his hand." The jurors began mumbling...

"Beautiee – I want to make sure the court understand you clearly – is it your testimony that you stabbed your husband in his hand?"

"Yes..."

"Hhmmmmm – if you were trying to kill your husband – you probably would've stabbed him somewhere else – somewhere there's a good chance he'd die..." The jurors began laughing, which angered Beverly...

"Objection!" Beverly yelled...

"Sustained..." Judge Duffey said... "The jury will disregard that last statement..." Judge Duffey said before Smalls continued...

"Beautiee – who left the house first after you had your altercation?"

"Bazil did..."

"So – to be clear – your husband left the house alive?"

"Yes..."

"Your honor – please enter this as an exhibit..." Smalls said as he handed it to Judge Duffey...

"So ordered..." Judge Duffey said and then it was entered into evidence...

"Beautiee – do you know what this is?" Smalls asked. I started crying as soon as I saw it...

"Yes..."

"Please tell the court what it is..."

"It's... the letter I wrote to Bazil... before I left him..." I answered as I broke down crying. Troy held Bazil's hand as he cried along with me...

"Pease read it to the jury..."

"Do I have to?"

"Yes Beautiee... please..."

"Hey my Thirst Quencher," I read before getting choked up. I blew my nose, wiped my tears, and started again... "I'm sorry I hurt you. I love you so much and if I had to marry you all over again, I would. When I married you, I promised you I'd love you forever... and I will... but I can't get that image of you and Trevor out of my head." I looked towards the back of the court room and saw Bazil was crying with me, which made me feel worse. I was just about out of tissues so I used what was left to wipe my nose instead of blowing it before I continued... "I thought I'd feel better after having sex with Trevor but to be honest, I feel like shit. I had sex with Trevor to hurt you because when I saw you with him it broke my heart – because I know you love him too – and I don't know if I can share you or your heart with anyone else. When you asked me to marry you, you promised me you'd make me feel good every day for the rest of my life – and you broke that promise." I had to stop again because I was getting choked up. Smalls tearing up along with some of the jurors, and Beverly could see that Judge Duffey was touched by what I'd read... "I'm back home. Please give me time. I'll call you when I'm ready. Love, Beautiee."

"I'm sorry Beautiee – I know that wasn't easy..." Smalls said...

"Objection!" Beverly said...

"Overruled..." Judge Duffey said...

"Beautiee – I have one last question for you..." Smalls said...

"Okay..."

"You really love your husband – don't you?"

"Yes..." I cried... "I love you Bazil..."

"I love you too..." Bazil cried as Beverly threw up her hands...

"I have no more questions..." Smalls said as he sat down...

"Mrs. Osgood – you're excused – that's it for today – we'll resume tomorrow at 9 a.m. sharp!" Judge Duffey said as he got up, put on his robe, and left the Bench. I watched as everyone left the court room. I turned to look at the back and Bazil was still sitting there...

"Let's go Beautiee..." the Bailiff said as he started walking towards me...

"Bazil..." I called out to stop him from leaving. Bazil turned around to look at me and I couldn't help myself – I ran right into his arms...

"Smalls – get a hold of your client!" The Bailiff yelled.

"She isn't going anywhere! She's right there in front of you!" Smalls yelled as he watched us...

"I'm sorry..." I cried as he held me...

"You have nothing to be sorry for…" Bazil said before he pulled me into a kiss…

"It's so hard…"

"I know…"

"I miss you…"

"I miss you too…"

"I love you Bazil…"

"I love you too… I'll see you tomorrow…" he said before he kissed me hard. "Please don't cry Beautiee…" he said as he kissed my tears…

"I don't wanna go back to jail…"

"I don't want you to go back either…"

"Beautiee – we gotta go…" Smalls said as he took my hand…

"Okay…" I whispered. The Bailiff came towards me and Bazil went out the court room door.

"How was court?" Mary asked when she saw me...

"It was okay..." I sighed...

"No it wasn't – I can tell by lookin' atcha – what happened?" she asked as she put her arm around me...

"Oh God..." I whispered as I started crying...

"The first day is always hard..." Mary said as she put my head on her shoulder and I continued to cry. Deputy Warden Hein walked over to us and I could see he wasn't too happy but in that moment – Mary was helping me hold it together – maybe she had ulterior motives – maybe she didn't – but I needed her...

"It's so hard..." I cried...

"I know..." Mary acknowledged as she touched my hair...

"I'm all alone in here – I can't see my husband - my friends can't come see me – my parents live down south – the only visit I get is from my attorney..." I cried...

"Why can't your husband come see you?"

"Because my husband is Bazil Osgood..."

"What'd you just say?"

"My husband is Bazil Osgood..."

"Hmmmmm... you'll be alright – I gotta go – hang in there..." she said as she got up and left me...

"Hmmmmm... musta been something I said..." I mumbled...

"That's exactly what it was..." Deputy Warden Hein said...

"Oh God – never mind – I don't even wanna know..." I sighed...

"Well just be careful with her – please!"

"Alright, alright... damn!"

"I'm serious Beautiee – it's for your protection!"

"What the fuck – sorry – what the hell – sorry – dammit – what am I supposed to do?"

"Here – take this – go back to your cell – and don't come out unless you wanna eat!" He snapped as he gave me a note pad and a pen.

"Thank you..." I whispered...

"You're welcome – I'll be leaving soon – I need to see you in my office – come with me..." he said as he pulled me up by my arm and took me down the corridor to his office. When we got to his office, he went in first and sat behind the desk... "Come inside and close the door..."

"Okay..." I said nervously as I closed the door...

"Come sit down in the chair by me..."

"Okay." I sat down and wondered what was going on as he picked up the phone and dialed a number...

"Here..." he said as he handed me the phone...

"Hello?"

"Beautiee..."

"Bazil!"

"You okay?"

"Noo...." I answered as I started crying...

"Please don't cry... you'll make me cry..."

"So..." I laughed.   Bazil laughed too.   "I love you...

"I love you too..."

"I'll see you tomorrow..."

"Yes... tomorrow..." I sighed... and then Bazil hung up." Thank you..." I said as I reached over to give Deputy Warden Hein a hug...

"Uh uh!"

"I'm sorry..."

"No offense — now let's get you back to your cell — and remember — don't come out unless you're hungry — hopefully this will all be over soon..." he said as he stood up. He waited for me to stand up and when I did, he took me by the arm, escorted me down the corridor, and back to my cell. I made myself comfortable, opened the pad, and starting writing to Bazil:

Love Me Baby

Lovin' at first sight, lovin' me alright,
Lovin' even when things ain't goin' right,
Lovin' me all night 'till the mornin' light,

Love Me Baby

Lovin' me in spite of my many faults,
Lovin' through the hurt, breakin' down my walls,
Lovin' on my heart, kissin' all my scars,

Love Me Baby

Lovin' every day when I've lost my way,
Lovin' me is hard, don't know what to say,
Lovin' let's me know that you wanna stay,

Love Me Baby

Lovin' me in spite of it being hot,
Lovin' all the while even when I'm not,
Lovin' in the dark 'till you find the spot,

Love Me Baby

Lovin' how you touch, and I'm feelin' good,
Lovin' by my side like I knew you could,
Lovin' all along 'till I understood,

Love Me Baby

I tore the song off the pad, folded it, put it in my
top pocket, and went to sleep.

Chapter 14

"Hey Smalls..." Bazil said as he opened the door..."

"Hey Bazil..." Smalls said as he came in and closed the door behind him...

"I read Beautiee's letter..."

"I know..."

"I can't let that stand..."

"Don't say another word Bazil..."

"That won't be necessary..."

"Oh God Bazil... what did you do?"

"Do you really wanna know?"

"As your attorney... should I know?"

"Yes... you should..."

"Okay Bazil... what happened?"

"I went to see Sergeant Chandler..."

"Oh God Bazil... please tell me you didn't..."

"I did..."

"Bazil!"

"I thanked him for handling this case with my wife professionally..."

"Oh shit... did he fall for that?"

"No... he felt my head and asked me if I was feeling okay..." Bazil laughed...

"So what did you do?"

"I told him I would never do anything to hurt my wife..."

"Oh I know he believed that..."

"Yes he did..."

"So while I was there... just like I predicted... Officer Thompson checked in..."

"Oh shit... Bazil..."

"He said he needed to use the bathroom before he headed back to Bridgeport... and it just so happens I needed to use the bathroom too... so I asked Sergeant Change to show me where the bathroom was... and I went..."

"Bazil... is Officer Thompson alive?"

"Absolutely... as I said... I would never do anything to hurt my wife..."

"What happened Bazil?"

"I pushed up on him... turned him around so he could see me kissing him on the back of his neck in the mirror..."

"Oh Shit! No the fuck you didn't!" Smalls laughed...

"Oh yes the fuck I did... and as I was kissing him I reached in his pants and grabbed his dick...grabbed his balls... squeezed... and asked him if he liked it..."

"Oh shit! What'd he say?"

"He begged me not to rape him!" Bazil laughed maniacally...

"Oh shit!" Smalls laughed...

"I asked him isn't that what you were going to do to my wife? Isn't that what you've been doing to all the female inmates?"

"Oh shit! He's been doing that to all the female inmates?"

"Yes..."

"How's he been getting away with it for so long?"

"None of them want to press charges..."

"I told your wife she should press charges — but she just wants to get out and come home..."

"She won't need to press charges..." Bazil laughed...

"Oh my God... Bazil what did you do?"

"I told him I have eyes and ears everywhere..."

"That's right... they still owe you..."

"Damn right they do!"

"So what he say after that..."

"I squeezed his dick and balls tighter... and I asked him if he liked having a dick or if he'd prefer a catheter..."

"Yoooo!" Smalls laughed... "That's some straight up gangster shit!"

"Exactly..."

"Oh shit... I forgot who I was talkin' too..."

"I told him if he ever touched my wife... or any other inmate... and it gets back to me... I'd find him... and I'd detach his dick and his balls from his body... and then I let him go... and he pissed himself!" Bazil laughed maniacally again...

"Oh shit!"

"Sergeant Chandler came into the bathroom and asked him what happened..."

"What'd he say?"

"He said he had an accident..."

"What the fuck did you do?!"

"I did what everyone should do after they use the bathroom... I washed my hands!"

"Bazil... I can't..." Smalls laughed...

"I called Deputy Warden Hein..."

"Bazil! I wish you hand't done that! If the court finds out – it could cause a miss-trial!"

"The only call I made to Deputy Warden Hein on the county phone was the one where I told him I needed to see my wife – he apologized – said there was nothing he could do – and hung up..."

"I thought you said you called Deputy Warden Hein?"

"Oh – my bad – I called Nathan..."

"Ooohhh...."

"He asked me if Officer Thompson was still alive... and I told him yes..."

"I'm thirsty..." Smalls said, changing the subject...

"I'll be right back – meet me in the living room..." Bazil said as he went to the kitchen and came back with two Heinekens...

"I have something for you..." Bazil said as he gave Smalls a Heineken... and the Bluetooth Cell Phone Recorder...

"What's this?"

"Proof I didn't kill MaryJane LaRue..."
"Will I need this in the future?"
"I hope not..."

Chapter 15

"All rise…"the Bailiff said. Everyone stood up. "Department One of the Superior Court is now in session. Judge Duffey presiding. Please be seated."

"Good morning, ladies and gentlemen" Judge Duffey said. "Calling the case of the People of the State of Connecticut versus Beautiee Osgood. Are both sides ready?"

"Ready for the People, Your Honor…" Beverly said.

"Ready for the Defense, Your Honor…" Smalls said.

"Mr. Osgood – what are you doing up here – did I not make myself clear?" he snapped as Bazil walked up to the front of the court room…

"Yes Your Honor – you made yourself perfectly clear…" Bazil answered as he walked up to the table where Smalls and I were sitting. The Bailiff stood up, waiting on Judge Duffey's instructions, but Bazil paid him no mind – he came over to me, pulled me up into a hug, and kissed me… "Good morning Beautiee…" he said after he kissed me.

"Good morning..." I breathed. Everyone watched and waited. Bazil let me go and I sat back down next to Smalls. Bazil walked to the back of the court room and sat down with Troy and Keisha. Beverly was annoyed but I didn't give a shit – I was too busy smiling. I took the song I wrote out my pocket and passed it to Smalls. Smalls read it, folded it, and put it in his pocket.

"Your Honor – please excuse me – I'll be right back..." Smalls said as he hurried out the court room. Judge Duffey watched as Smalls left the court room and kept looking to see if Bazil would get up to follow him, but Bazil didn't. Smalls went out into the hallway, took out his cell phone, and read a text from his wife, Josefina, and called her right away... "I got your message – Judge Duffey doesn't like to be kept waiting – I'll call you as soon as I can – I love you too..." he said before hanging up. When he came back into the court room he saw Judge Duffey stop to look at his watch and used the opportunity to drop the folded paper in Bazil's lap as he walked towards the table...

"Is everything alright?" Judge Duffey asked...

"Yes Your Honor – thanks for asking..." Smalls answered as he sat down next to me...

"Do you need a recess?"

"No Your Honor..."

"Does anyone else need to be excused? Does anyone need to use the bathroom? All good? Good – Beverly – please call your next witness..."

"I'm re-calling Detective Katina Jones..." Beverly said as she stood up. Bazil started reading as Katina took the stand...

"Please state your name for the record..." Judge Duffey instructed...

"Katina Jones."

"Please raise your right hand and place your left hand on the bible..." Judge Duffey instructed as the court clerk held the Bible... "Do you swear, under penalty of perjury, that the testimony you are about to give shall be the truth, the whole truth, and nothing but the truth?"

"I do..." Detective Jones said as she sat down.

"Very well – Beverly – you may proceed..."

"What's wrong?" Troy whispered as tears fell from Bazil's eyes. Bazil didn't say anything – he just kept reading...

"Detective Jones – please tell us what happened when you were called to the defendant's home on January 13, 2019..."

"An ambulance was dispatched to the defendant's home. An attempted homicide was called in along with two other homicides. I was the first to arrive on the scene."

"Could you describe it for us?"

"It was horrific. There was blood everywhere. The neighbors were in the bedroom with the defendant. At first, I couldn't tell who was bleeding or who shot who."

"Do you see the neighbors in the court?"

"Yes."

"Could you point them out for the jury?" Detective Jones pointed to the back of the court room at Troy and Keisha. "Your Honor – please note that Detective Jones pointed out Troy and Keisha Cochran."

"So noted – continue..." Judge Duffey acknowledged.

"Please tell us what happened next..." Beverly said...

"When I got there I was questioning the officers outside. As I was questioning them, they were loading Bazil Osgood's body onto the stretcher and into the ambulance. They closed the door to the ambulance and started to drive off. Mrs. Osgood came running out wearing a robe. She was screaming for Mr. Osgood and I could see she was covered in blood. She pushed me down and kept screaming for Mr. Osgood and kept running towards the ambulance. The ambulance stopped, she got in, and they drove off."

"You testified the defendant pushed you – is that correct?"

"Yes."

"Did you feel threatened by the defendant?"

"No."

"Okay what happened next?"

"I went into the house and their neighbor, Troy Cochran, was in the bedroom."

"Were you able to question him?"

"No."

"Why not?"

"He wouldn't answer any questions."

"Did he offer an explanation?"

"No he didn't."

"So you weren't able to question him."

"Not at that moment."

"What happened next?"

"I began questioning the officers and I noticed two more bodies and a gun."

"Please tell the court who the deceased victims are."

"Sonia Santos and Trevor Joseph."

"Is this the gun you recovered from the crime scene?"

"Yes – that's the gun..."Katina answered as the gun was entered into evidence. I tried to hold it together but as soon as I saw the gun I began crying uncontrollably. Smalls did his best to console me but it was to no avail, so he just held me and let me cry. Bazil stood up and the Bailiff stood up right along with him. Troy touched Bazil to get him to sit back down.

"Who's fingerprints were on the gun?"

"The defendant's fingerprints were on the gun."

"What happened next?"

"The Coroner took the bodies to the morgue, the officers continued to process the crime scene, and I left to go the hospital."

"Your Honor – may I share the crime scene photos with the jury?"

"Bailiff – please share the crime scene photos with the jury..." Judge Duffey ordered. The Bailiff took a copy of the photos and shared them with the jury. Smalls continued to hold me as I cried. After the jury finished looking at the photos, the Bailiff took the copies and gave them back to Beverly...

"Detective – what happened when you got to the hospital?"

"I saw the defendant's neighbor, Keisha Cochran, and I asked her if I could get a statement.

"Was she cooperative?"

"Yes she was."

"Were you ever able to question her husband?"

"Yes."

"In your opinion – do you believe their statements are truthful?"

"Hole up – don't be calling me a liar!" Keisha blurted out from the back of the court room...

"Order in the court!" Judge Duffey snapped. "I will not tolerate outbursts from anyone in this court – unless you are called to the witness stand – you are to be quiet!"

"Sorry Your Honor..." Keisha said.

"Yes – I believe their statements are truthful..." Detective Jones answered.

"Were you able to get a statement from the defendant?"

"No – she refused to speak to me without her attorney..."

"Hmmmmm... I'm not surprised..."

"Objection!" Smalls yelled...

"Sustained..." Judge Duffey acknowledged.

"Your witness..." Beverly said as she sat down...

"Are you okay?" Smalls asked me...

"No..."

"I'll be right here..."

"I know..." I said as he went up to the stand...

"Hello Katina..."

"Good morning..."

"You testified the defendant pushed you – is that correct?"

"Objection – asked and answered!" Beverly snapped.

"Smalls – are you going somewhere?" Judge Duffey asked...

"Yes Your Honor..."

"I'll allow it – objection overruled..." Judge Duffey ordered...

"You could have placed the defendant under arrest at that moment – but you didn't – why?"

"I knew she wasn't going anywhere..."

"So – to be clear – you knew she wasn't running?"

"Yes."

"You testified that you were able to get a statement from the neighbors – and you also testified that you believed their statements were truthful – is that correct?"

"Yes."

"Your Honor – may I share the neighbor's statements with the jury?"

"Bailiff – please share the statements with the jury..." Judge Duffey ordered. The Bailiff used a projector to put their statements on screen. The statements were clear and legible to the jury. The judge allowed the jury a few minutes to read the statements before Smalls continued...

"Is it true that you bagged and tagged their neighbor, Keisha Cochran's clothes into evidence?"

"Yes."

"Did you find blood on the clothes?"

"Yes."

"Who did the blood belong to?"

"The blood belonged to Bazil Osgood, Sonia Santos, and Trevor Joseph."

"You testified you were in the bedroom of the defendant's home – is that correct?"

"Yes."

"You also testified that the officers continued to process the crime scene – is that correct?"

"Yes."

"To your knowledge – is there a bathroom in the defendant's bedroom?"

"Yes – there is."

"What - if anything – was recovered from the bathroom?"

"DNA was recovered that matched the defendant as well as her husband."

"Could you be more specific?'"

"We recovered semen matching Bazil Osgood and hair matching the defendant and Bazil Osgood."

"Did you recover any blood?"

"No we did not."

"So – to be clear – my client has been charged with the attempted murder of her husband – the murder of Sonia Santos – the murder of Trevor Joseph – my client had blood on her from her husband as well as the other victims – they have a master bathroom – and you didn't recover a single drop of blood from the bathroom?"

"No we did not."

"So – based on your testimony – my client did not try and take a shower to wash away evidence – instead – she ran outside to jump in the ambulance with her husband – is that correct?"

"That's correct."

"Hmmmmm - thank you – I have no further questions..." Smalls said with a smile as he sat down. "You okay?" Smalls whispered to me. I didn't answer – I just shook my head no...

"Court's in recess – be back in 15 minutes..." Judge Duffey said as he stood up and left the bench. The Bailiff escorted the jurors to the waiting room and Troy, Keisha, and Bazil went out into the hallway.

"C'mon..." Smalls said as he got up and waited for me. He took me by the hand, and we walked out into the hallway...

"Beautiee..." Bazil said as he pulled me into his arms. The Bailiffs were going to object but once we started crying they just stood there watching. Troy, Keisha, and Smalls hugged us both as we held each other and cried...

"We gotchall..." Troy said as he started crying...

"Don't start that shit Troy..." Keisha sniffed...

"This some bullshit!" Troy snapped...

"I know – shit – here comes the Bailiff..." Smalls said. The Bailiff walked towards us, stopped to observe, then went towards the men's room...

"I love the song..." Bazil said before he pulled me into a kiss...

"And I love you..." I said before I kissed him back...

"Promise me you'll sing it to me when you get home..." he breathed before he kissed me again...

"I promise..." I said as we continued kissing...

"Ahem!" The Bailiff interrupted. We all turned around to look at the Bailiff. "Judge Duffey's waiting..." he said.

"Oh okay – let's go..." Smalls said as he took my hand and pulled me into the court room and up to the table. Bazil, Troy, and Keisha came into the court room and sat down in the back.

"All rise..."the Bailiff said. Everyone stood up. "Department One of the Superior Court is now in session. Judge Duffey presiding. Please be seated."

"Calling the case of the People of the State of Connecticut versus Beautiee Osgood. Are both sides ready?"

"Ready for the People, Your Honor..." Beverly said.

"Ready for the Defense, Your Honor..." Smalls said.

"Beverly – are you ready to call your next witness?" Judge Duffey asked.

"Yes Your Honor."

"Very well – you may call your next witness..."

"Thank you Your Honor – I call Beautiee Osgood."

"Please state your name for the record..." Judge Duffey instructed...

"Beautiee Osgood."

"Please raise your right hand and place your left hand on the bible…" Judge Duffey instructed as the court clerk held the bible… "Do you swear, under penalty of perjury, that the testimony you are about to give shall be the truth, the whole truth, and nothing but the truth?"

"I will…" I said as I sat down.

"Very well – Beverly – you may proceed…"

"Mrs. Osgood – please tell the court what happened on the night of January 13, 2019…"

"I invited Sonia Santos over."

"Why did you invite Sonia over?"

"You already know why she was invited over."

"Your Honor – Permission to Treat The Witness Hostile!" Beverly snapped!

"Permission granted – you may proceed…" Judge Duffey acknowledged…

"Mrs. Osgood – I'm going to ask you again…" she said as she walked up to the bench to get closer to my face… "WHY DID YOU INVITE SONIA SANTOS TO YOUR HOME?" I started waiving my hand to shoo her away from me. Smalls was shaking his head no but I didn't care…

"Could you back up please?" I asked sarcastically…

"Your Honor!" Beverly snapped before she was interrupted…

"Mrs. Osgood – answer the question!" Judge Duffey snapped…

176

"Your Honor – I have no problem answering questions – but she needs to back up – her breath stinks!" Everyone bust out laughing and Judge Duffey was not amused... "Order in the fucking court – now! Mrs. Osgood – let me warn you – today is not the day to test me – do I make myself clear?"

"Yes Your Honor – I meant no disrespect – I'm sorry..." I said as I put my head down...

"I'm not the one you need to apologize too..." Judge Duffey said as he pointed to Beverly...

"I'm sorry – I didn't mean to offend you..." I lied...

"Apology accepted – please answer the question..." she said as she backed up. I could see she was pissed off and I knew I had her where I wanted her...

"I invited Sonia over to have sex with me while my husband watched." The jurors gasped. Troy and Keisha had their mouths open in shock.

"And Sonia agreed to this?"

"Yes."

"You're lying right now – aren't you?" I could see the anger was building in her. Smalls looked at me pleading with his eyes not to lose my cool – but I knew what I was doing...

"I'm not lying..."

"You really expect the court to believe you invited Sonia over to have sex with you – and she knew your husband was in the closet – and she was okay with that?"

"Yes."

"Hmmmmm – too bad we can't ask Sonia – isn't it?"

"Objection..." Smalls said.

"Sustained..." Judge Duffey acknowledged...

"Did your husband participate?"

"Yes he did."

"And it was consensual?"

"Yes it was."

"You're lying – it wasn't consensual at all – you set your husband up so you could kill him..."

"Stop it! That's not true!" Bazil yelled...

"Bailiff – remove him from the court room – now!" Judge Duffey ordered. Bazil got up and left the court room before the Bailiff could reach him, but he stood outside so he could continue listening. The Bailiff stood in the back of the court room to make sure Bazil didn't come back in as Beverly continued...

"How did Trevor get in your house?"

"I don't know."

"Isn't it true that you invited him?"

"No I didn't."

"Would you change your answer if I told you we have surveillance of Trevor, in fact, letting himself in and not breaking in?"

"My answer wouldn't change – I didn't invite Trevor to my home."

"What happened – in your words?"

"Sonia agreed to come to the house. We had some wine, we went upstairs to the bedroom, and we started having sex."

"Where was your husband?"

"He was in the closet watching."

"Did he stay in the closet?"

"No."

"So he came out the closet – then what happened?"

"He had sex with me."

"Hmmmmm – interesting – so you had no idea that Trevor was in the closet?"

"No."

"When did you realize Trevor was in the closet?"

"When I was on my back."

"On your back?"

"Yes – I was on my back on the bed."

"And where was Sonia?"

"She was on top of me."

"Hmmmmm – and where was your husband?"

"He was on my right side."

"And he didn't know Trevor was in the closet?"

"No."

"Okay – so when did you see Trevor?"

"I saw the gun first – I screamed for Bazil to watch out..." I said as I started to cry... "But Bazil didn't move fast enough... Oh God!" I cried...

"Is that when your husband was shot?"

"Yes…"

"What happened next?"

"I realized it was Trevor when he stepped out of the closet… he pointed the gun… I thought he was pointing it at both of us so I pulled Sonia down on top of me… Sonia got shot in the back – Trevor dropped the gun – he said it was all my fault – he said Sonia didn't deserve to die – he pulled Sonia off me and hugged her – I picked up the gun – and I shot him!" I cried. The jurors gasped…

"So – let me get this straight – are you telling us that Trevor let himself in your house – snuck in your closet with a gun – shot your husband – shot Sonia – dropped the gun – blamed you for it all – and then pulled Sonia off of you – instead of finishing the job and shooting you too?"

"Yeeesss!" I cried…

"Nice try Mrs. Osgood – but the truth is you invited Trevor to your home along with Sonia – you got them to let their guard down – you shot your husband – you shot Sonia – and you shot Trevor too – isn't that what really happened? Isn't it?"

"Noooo…." I cried…

"I have no further questions!" Beverly said as she sat down… "Your witness!" she said as she flung up her hands…

"Your Honor – may I be excused to get my client some water?" Smalls asked….

"No you may not be excused – if your client needs some water the Bailiff can get it – please continue…" Judge Duffey ordered…

"Yes Your Honor – Beautiee – are you okay to continue?"

"Yes…"

"Did you shoot your husband?"

"Noooo…." I cried…

"Did you shoot Sonia?"

"Nooo…"

"Did you shoot Trevor?"

"Yes…"

"Why?"

"Because he shot Bazil and he was going to shoot me…"

"Is it your testimony that you believe Trevor was going to shoot you if you didn't shoot him?"

"Yes…."

"Did you invite Trevor to your house?"

"No!" I cried.

"No further questions…" Smalls said as he sat back down…

"Courts in recess – we're closed for lunch – everyone be back at 1pm sharp!" Judge Duffey snapped before he stood up and left the bench. Smalls got up from the table and I got up to follow him out the court room. Troy and Keisha were already in the hall with Bazil when we got there…

"Bazil…" I cried as I fell into his arms…

"Break it up..." the Bailiff ordered – but we ignored him.

"My client isn't doing anything wrong – leave her alone..." Smalls said as he stood in front of us...

"Either they break it up – or I make sure Judge Duffey has you removed as counsel!" the Bailiff growled...

"I'll go..." Bazil said as he let me go...

"You can't leave – you're up after lunch..."

"Excuse me?" Smalls asked.

"Check your witness list – he's up after lunch..." the Bailiff said. Smalls checked his list and saw the Bailiff was correct. "That's why I told y'all to break it up – you can't conversate before you give testimony..."

"You could'a just told me that!" Smalls snapped.

"You're right – I could've – see you at 1pm sharp..." he laughed as we walked off...

"Yo – that shit right there – mutha fucka!" Troy yelled...

"Troy – keep it down..." Keisha said...

"Fuck him!" Troy snapped...

"I know – but Beautiee needs us right now – we can't afford to lose it – she can't afford it..." Smalls said...

"Fuck this – yo Bazil – let's go outside a minute..." Troy said as he stormed off...

"Don't mind him – he gets like that when someone he cares about is being mistreated..." Keisha explained.

"I know – I love y'all..." I said...

"We love you too..." Keisha said...

"Yo Bazil – this is fucked up..." Troy said...

"I fucked up..." Bazil said as he started crying...

"C'mon Bazil – don't start that shit man..." Troy said as he started tearing up...

"I can't stand to see her hurting like this... I just want to protect her... and I can't..."

"Stop talkin'..." Troy said as he saw the Bailiff walk by...

"I haven't eaten yet – let's go across the street..." Bazil said as he started across the street and Troy followed...

"Shit – where the hell did Troy go – oh that's him calling me – bye y'all – she said as she left...

"C'mon..." Smalls said as he took me to the attorney-client room... "Sit down..." he said as I sat down and then he sat down across from me... "Le'me ask you something – and be honest..."

"Okay..."

"Did Beverly's breath really stink?"

"A little..."

"Oh shit..." he laughed... "You were serious?"

"I said that to piss her off... and it worked..."

"Whhaaattt?"

"I did it on purpose... she played right into my hands... and the jury bought it... hook, line, and sinker!" I laughed as I banged my hand on the table...

"Beautiee... did you lie?"

"Smalls?"

"Yes?"

"Do you really believe I lied on the stand?"

"No... at least I don't want to believe that... but..."

"But Beverly is the Bitch that's trying to put me away – I didn't lie – all I did – all she did – was show the jury who she really is..."

"You hungry?"

"Yea..."

"Okay – I'ma go get us some lunch – I'll be right back – please – whatever you do – don't leave this room!"

"Alright, alright!" I said as he ran out to get us lunch...

"Shit – I gotta pee – I'ma go to the bathroom right quick..."

"Hey Smalls – where's Beautiee?" Bazil asked when he saw Smalls walk inside the restaurant...

"She's waiting for me in the attorney-client conference room..." he answered as he picked up a menu...

"I'ma go holla at her right quick before everyone gets back..." Bazil said as he hurried towards the door...

"Don't get caught!" Smalls yelled... but Bazil was already across the street...

"Is that door opened?" Bazil heard the Bailiff ask someone as he went to the end of the hallway...

"Yea – it's still open..." they answered. Bazil hid in the corner so nobody would see him. He watched and waited for the Bailiff to come out. When he saw the Bailiff didn't lock the door, he hurried down to the attorney-client waiting room to look for me but I was still in the bathroom so he hurried down the hall and waited...

Twisted Beautiee Tree

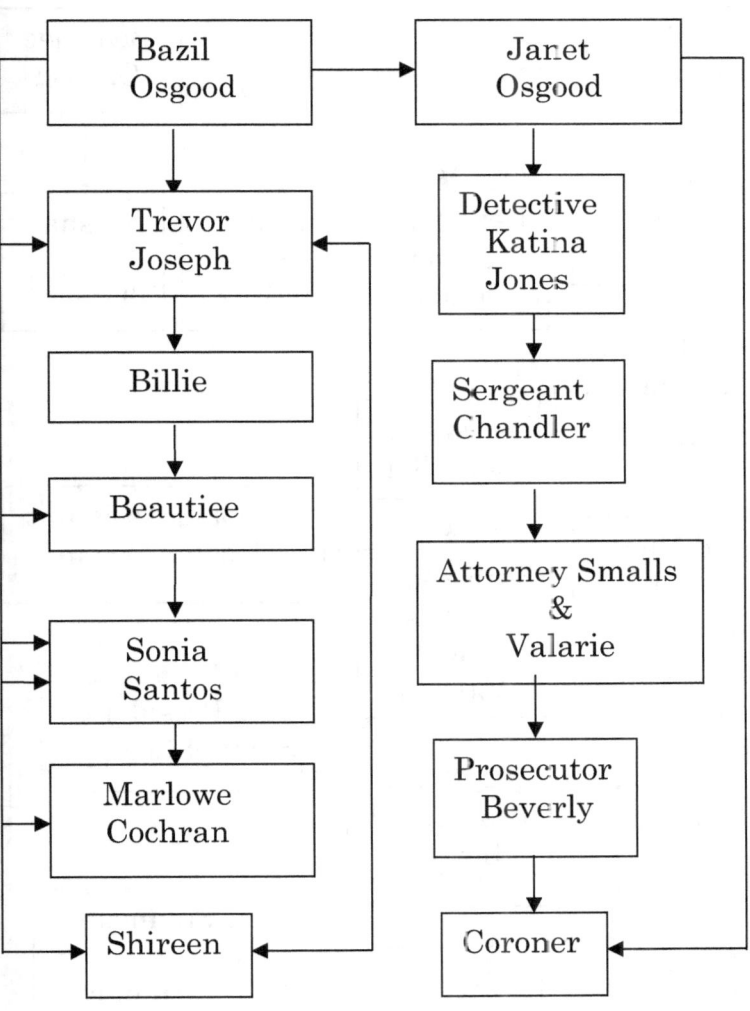

Twisted Beautiee Tree

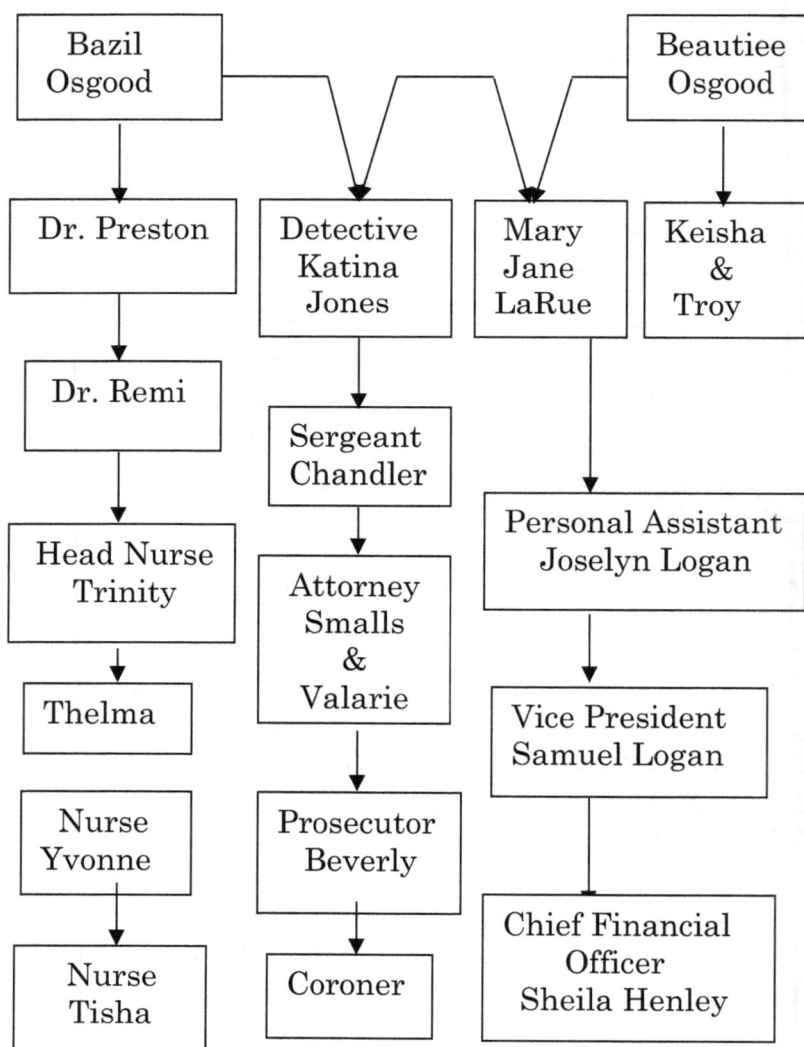